WORD NERD

SUSIN
NIELSEN

TUNDRA BOOKS

Published in Canada by Tundra Books,
75 Sherbourne Street, Toronto, Ontario M5A 2P9

Published in the United States by Tundra Books of Northern New York,
P.O. Box 1030, Plattsburgh, New York 12901

Library of Congress Control Number: 2007938541

Library and Archives Canada Cataloguing in Publication

Nielsen-Fernlund, Susin, 1964-
    Word nerd / Susin Nielsen.

Ages 9 and above.
ISBN 978-0-88776-875-0

    I. Title.
PS8577.I37W67 2008   jC813'.54   C2007-906100-1

We acknowledge the financial support of the Government of Canada
through the Book Publishing Industry Development Program (BPIDP) and
that of the Government of Ontario through the Ontario Media Development
Corporation's Ontario Book Initiative.

We further acknowledge the support of the Canada Council for the Arts and
the Ontario Arts Council for our publishing program.

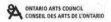

ONTARIO ARTS COUNCIL
CONSEIL DES ARTS DE L'ONTARIO

Design: Kelly Hill

Typeset in Scala

Printed and bound in Canada

1 2 3 4 5 6   13 12 11 10 09 08

MOM

To my mom, Eleanor Nielsen,
for her unconditional love;
and for being the one person
I can always beat at Scrabble.

ACKNOWLEDGMENTS

Special thanks to Val Gallant and all the members of the Vancouver Scrabble Club for letting me be a fly on the wall at their regular meetings and at the Vancouver Scrabble Tournament. Unlike my fictional characters, I never had the courage to play a game against any of them. Thanks must also go to Stefan Fatsis, author of *Word Freak*, a rollicking good read about the world of competitive Scrabble.

I also owe undying gratitude to

Susan Juby, whose generosity knows no bounds;

Hilary McMahon, both for taking me on and for her day-to-day passion and dedication;

Kathy Lowinger and Sue Tate, for seeing the potential, and for their excellent notes that helped make the story stronger and better;

Luther Wright, my "longest" friend, who kindly let me use his lyrics for "Darlin'";

My husband, Goran, who read an early draft of the manuscript and told me I wasn't crazy;

And last but not least, my son, Oskar, who let me read the manuscript aloud to him – not once but twice – and who, after giving me some perceptive dialogue notes, told me it was his favorite book, both times.

L G R Y A L E

early, ale, all, gall, gel, leg, real, gear, largely, lag, gale

ALLERGY

he day I almost died, the sky was a bright, brilliant blue – a nice change from the rain earlier in the week. A few clouds hung over the North Shore mountains, but they were far away.

I was sitting at a picnic table on the school grounds, eating my lunch. Being mid-October, it wasn't really warm enough to eat outside, but I preferred it to the lunchroom, which was noisy and crowded and occasionally hazardous to my health if some kid tried to trip

me. Sometimes a guy could feel lonelier surrounded by people than he could when he was alone.

I had another bite of my sandwich, then looked down at my feet. I was wearing my brand-new sneakers. Only the keenest eye would be able to tell they weren't Nikes. Mom could never afford Nikes, but when she'd taken me to Chinatown on the weekend, I'd spotted a knockoff brand that was practically identical and a quarter of the price.

They looked good, my new shoes. Really good. Bright white, with a navy blue swish on the side and matching navy laces. In retrospect, I shouldn't have worn my neon orange socks with them, but even so, they looked mighty fine. They almost made me forget about my pants, which were getting too short, but as Mom liked to say, she wasn't made of money. New pants would have to wait.

On the field, Troy, Mike, and Josh were kicking a soccer ball around. For a moment I thought about asking if I could join them, but the last time I tried that they made me the goalie, then kicked the ball at my head over and over again until I had a headache. So I decided to stay put.

The sun felt good, and I closed my eyes. I could feel the warm rays on my face and imagined them zapping the blackheads on my nose into oblivion.

Then the sun disappeared and something bounced

hard off my head. I opened my eyes. The first thing I saw was the soccer ball, rolling away from me. The second thing I saw were three sets of big Nike-clad feet.

I looked up. Troy, Mike, and Josh were towering over me, blocking the sun.

"*Oops*," said Troy. He was the tallest of the three by at least a head and as broad as a tree trunk. He had short, thick black hair and his eyes were too small for his face.

"It's okay. Accidents happen," I said, even though accidents between their soccer ball and my cranium occurred at least three times a week.

"What's for lunch, Spambrose?" asked Mike, who was what some people would call stocky and I would call fat. He had curly brown hair and a permanent scowl, and his jeans hung way below his waist, exposing a good four inches of his underwear, which I understood was supposed to look not dorky but cool.

"Ambrose," I answered. "Cheese sandwich, carrots, apple –"

"Your lunch sucks," Mike said.

I laughed. It came out like a horse's whinny because, I confess, I was forcing it a bit. "Yeah, my mom's big on nutrition. . . ."

"Hey, Damnbrose, is it true you're allergic to peanuts?" asked Troy.

"Ambrose. Yeah, it's true."

"I've been going to this school for, like, six years. For six years, I've eaten peanut butter and jam sandwiches for lunch. Then you show up, and suddenly our school's declared a peanut-free zone."

"Yeah, my mom takes it pretty seriously. Have you ever tried almond butter? Because it's not a bad substitute. . . ."

"Look at his shoes," said Josh. He was the smallest of the three, but strong and wiry and tough, and his hair was shaved into a kind of Mohawk. For some reason, he scared me the most.

Troy and Mike looked at my feet.

"Ike," said Troy.

"It's pronounced *Ikee*," I explained. "Like *Nike* without the *N*."

Troy shook his head. "You are such a freak."

The good feeling I'd had about my new shoes started to fade.

"Close your eyes," said Josh.

"Why?"

"Because I said."

Now this made me a little nervous because the last time I'd closed my eyes for them, I'd opened them to find a dead crow in my lap.

But it's very hard to say no to the Three Stooges. I called them that (only in my head and never out loud because I am not suicidal) because my mom had taken me to a "Three Stooges Marathon" a few years ago and we'd watched their old shows about four hours straight. Troy was Moe, the leader; Mike was Larry; and Josh was Curly because his hair was cut so short, he almost looked bald.

It didn't really make sense because the Three Stooges were funny. Troy, Mike, and Josh were one hundred percent not.

So I closed my eyes, and to pass the time I scrambled the letters from "Three Stooges" in my head to see what new words I could make. I came up with *ghettos*, *together*, *shooters*, *shortest*, and had just figured out *soothers* when Josh said, "Okay, you can open your eyes."

I did. Nothing was in my lap. I patted my hair. Nothing – no worms, no spit.

"What'd you guys do?" I asked.

But Troy just patted me on the back, a little too hard. "See you, Peanut-butter-and-Jambrose."

"Ambrose," I said. "See you guys in math."

They walked away. I picked up my sandwich and took a bite, thinking that, all things considered, my chat with the Three Stooges had gone pretty well. In fact, I was thinking that maybe this was a step forward in our relationship when suddenly I felt itchy all over, followed by a distinct tightening in my throat.

5

I knew that feeling. It had been eight long years, but I still knew. I peeled back the bread on the top of my sandwich and, sure enough, there it was.

A peanut. Well, to be accurate: half a peanut. The other half was in my digestive tract, and I was going into anaphylactic shock. All the mucous membranes in my throat were swelling up and I could hardly breathe. I reached for my EpiPen, then I remembered that it wasn't with me. It was in a fanny pack in my locker, where I hid it most mornings, even though my mom would kill me if she knew. When I wore the fanny pack, the Three Stooges called me a fag because it was hot pink – a free sample my mom got at a shopping mall in Kelowna, where we'd lived until two months ago.

So the shot that could have saved my life was inside and two floors up, and I was outside in the school-yard gasping for breath. I caught sight of Troy, Mike, and Josh doubled over with laughter as they watched me. Just before everything went black, I pictured the headline of my obituary: FRIENDLESS NERD KILLED BY PEANUT. And the byline: DIES WEARING IKES.

C T T P O E R

pet, poet, rope, pore, opt, top, pot, potter, core, tore

P R O T E C T

But I didn't die. Instead, I had what the doctor called a near-death experience, which, I guess, sounds kind of exciting, but I personally wouldn't recommend it.

I didn't see a bright blazing light. I didn't see God, or Allah, or Buddha. My life didn't flash before my eyes. In fact, after I blacked out, I didn't remember anything until the ambulance attendant gave me the first shot of adrenaline, which is enough to wake anyone up. After that, I must have passed out again because when I woke up, I was in a hospital bed and my mom was sitting beside me, wearing the floppy hat with the flower on it that I had bought her last Christmas from Value Village. She was clutching my hand, bawling her eyes out.

I wanted to tell her I was okay, that everything was going to be okay, but my throat felt funny and I think I was drugged because I couldn't get the words out. This bothered me because I could see how upset she was.

I love my mom. She has tried to protect me my whole life, and not just from peanuts. When I was little and we still lived in Edmonton, Nana Ruth used to joke that our place was outfitted like an asylum – all that was missing were the straitjackets. Our outlets were plugged with wall-socket protectors; medicines and cleaning products were locked up; sharp-edged tables were padded with hunks of foam; drawers and cupboards all had childproof locks. We even had big plastic clip-locks to hold the toilet seat down because Mom was worried that I might lift up the seat, fall in, and drown.

She made me watch the "Stranger Danger" video twenty thousand times. I've never been allowed to climb ladders or trees, or swim unless she's in the pool, and she still makes me hold her hand when we cross busy roads. Sometimes it's a little embarrassing, especially when she swears at bad drivers in a loud voice from the sidewalk, but I know her heart is in the right place.

Because my mom has done such a good job protecting me, I decided, when we moved to Vancouver two months ago, that I was old enough to return the favor. That's why I've told her that everything's working out well in my seventh-grade classroom at Cypress Elementary; that I have friends, and their names are Troy, Mike, and Josh. I can see how happy it makes her, because in Edmonton, Regina, and Kelowna, I never really had friends.

And what would be the point in telling her that this school was the same as all the rest? That, on a good day, the Three Stooges called me names; that, on a bad day, they threw my lunch into the toilet and, on one occasion, my lunch *and* my gym shorts.

The thing is, I've learned to live with it. It's not the end of the world. And besides, if I told my mom the truth, she would flip. She would make a big production out of it. The principal would be called, parents would be called . . . and when it all simmered down, who would be left to deal with the ugly aftermath? Me.

And, to be honest, it made me feel better when I could tell her stories at the end of the day that made it sound like I had a life:

"Then we all shot hoops at lunch."

"I helped Mike with his math after school."

"Troy invited me to his birthday party at Planet Lazer."

That last one almost backfired. I'd chosen laser tag because I knew my mom thought it was violent and dangerous, so I was shocked when she said I could go. We picked out a gift, and Mom took me by bus to Planet Lazer, which took over an hour because it was all the way out in Richmond. When we got there, she wanted to come in and meet Troy's mom, but I begged her not to, saying it wouldn't look cool. She finally backed down.

For the next three hours, I stayed in the laser-tag bathroom because it was pouring rain outside. I read the book we'd bought for Troy – *The Thief Lord* by Cornelia Funke – and, for a while, I could really believe that I was in Venice, Italy, on an incredible adventure and not in a stinky cubicle perched on a toilet seat.

On the way home, the bus was crowded and people were wet, so it smelled like dampness and armpits. Mom and I had to stand near the front.

"So? How was it?" she asked.

"Great. Our team won. I shot a laser right through Troy's heart."

She shook her head. "*Ugh*, it sounds awful. You didn't eat the cake, did you?"

"No, Mom," I said. "I didn't eat anything except the snack you sent me with."

After that, we were both quiet. I watched the rain swirl down the bus windows like miniature rivers and snuck peeks at the unsmiling faces around me.

This time, the lie hadn't felt very good. It hadn't made me feel like I had a life.

It just made me feel like a speck in the universe.

I must've drifted back to sleep because the next time I woke up, I could hear my mom in the hospital corridor, talking to a doctor. Her voice was raised about an octave. I could picture her in her hat, waving her arms around, and I felt a twinge of pity for the doctor. Suddenly I heard, crystal clear: "They slipped a peanut into his sandwich? *His school friends intentionally slipped a peanut into his sandwich?*"

Oh, man. I wondered who had dared to snitch on the Three Stooges. *Another kid who'd seen what had happened? Or, perhaps, one of the Three Stooges themselves, in a rare moment of guilt?*

Then a hazy memory floated to the surface of my brain, and I groaned. A pretty nurse had been standing over me when they gave me my second shot of adrenaline. She'd asked me what had happened. . . .

And I'd told her everything. It was me. I was the snitch.

In the hallway, my mom was still shouting and, crazy as it sounds, at that moment, I wasn't thinking about how grateful I was to be alive.

I was thinking, *Why didn't that peanut just kill me?*

Because I knew with absolute certainty that the poop was about to hit the fan.

— 3 —

R O Y S H T I

his, hit, sh—, stir, toy, soy, shot, hot, shirt, short, story

HISTORY

We found out I had a peanut allergy when I was three years old. We were living in Edmonton, and my mom decided to take a part-time teaching job at the university because we were running out of money from the life insurance policy. She put me in a home daycare run by a woman named Betty Spooner (*snooper, opens, peon, pores, poser, prone, prose, ropes, spore, person*). I don't remember much about Betty except that she was prehistoric – like, she looked ninety-seven, but maybe she was only sixty.

Betty Spooner hadn't kept up to date on allergies in kids because on my second week there, she served PB&J sandwiches for lunch. I took a couple of bites and, lucky for me, Betty happened to glance up from the soap opera she was watching on the little black-and-white TV she kept in the kitchen and noticed I was swelling up like a puffer fish. She called 911 and then my mom. At the hospital, the doctor told my mom that I had a severe allergy to peanuts and that if I ever ate one again, the reaction could be even worse. That's when I got the EpiPen and my very own MedicAlert bracelet, which I used to think was cool but which I now hate.

Anyway, I didn't go back to Betty Spooner's. I heard my mom screaming at her on the phone that night and calling her a half-wit, which, in retrospect, wasn't very fair. Betty didn't know any better, but my mom is – well, that's my mom. After that, she didn't want anyone else to look after me, so she quit her teaching job and stayed home with me full-time until I started school.

But even when she was looking after me full-time, my mom still didn't feel I was safe. I have a vivid memory of going to the playground near our apartment, the one with the rusty red monkey bars, and an old man was sitting on a bench, feeding peanuts in their shells to the squirrels. I picked up a shell and almost put it in my mouth. Mom whacked it out of my hand just in time, then she lectured the old man about peanut allergies, and he wound up calling her a *puta* (which I found out much later means "prostitute." Which she isn't. She doesn't even date).

After that, she bought me one of those kid-harnesses, which I had to wear wherever we went. I still remember running down the street, or through a mall, and being yanked gently back when I ran out of leash. I also remember Mom getting into arguments with strangers who thought putting a kid on a leash was cruel. When that happened, I'd pretend I was a dog and bark, and that usually made them go away. Once I even licked my mom's hand, but she didn't like that very much.

Nana Ruth, who still visited us a lot in those days, couldn't stand to see me wear the harness. She and Mom had heated arguments about it when they thought I was asleep.

"It's not right, Irene. I know you want to protect him, but this is going too far."

"Get off my back, Mom, please. I'm just trying to keep him safe."

I loved Nana Ruth, with her powdery white hair and her brightly colored tracksuits, but I also loved my mom, and hearing them fight made my stomach hurt.

Nana Ruth didn't win that argument. I kept wearing the leash.

Right up to kindergarten.

But in case I'm painting my mom to be a nutcase, she isn't. At least, not so much.

In fact, she was this close to being a normal mom, and we were this close to being a normal family, with two parents and me, and who knows? Maybe a brother or a sister, or at least a pet.

My mom and dad really loved each other. He was a handsome, tanned Australian who had come to Canada on a work visa. He'd headed straight to Banff to work as a ski instructor and he only meant to stay a year. My mom was a tiny thing, with long brown hair pulled back in a ponytail, and she wore granny glasses, which made her look serious and older than her twenty-five years. She had just finished getting her Ph.D. in English literature at the University of Calgary, where she'd written a thesis called "The Effects of an Isolated Upbringing on the Imaginations of the Brontë Sisters." It got published in a journal somewhere, even though (no offense to my mom intended) it didn't exactly sound like a page-turner.

She had gone to Banff for a week with a girlfriend to blow off steam and celebrate, and she met my dad one night at a pub. According to my mom, he shouldn't have been her type at all. "I was all brains, he was all brawn." She would smile when I asked her to recount the story, which I did quite often.

And yet, they fell head over heels in love. Within months, my dad moved to Calgary, and soon afterward they got married. They rented a bungalow just three blocks from Nana Ruth's apartment. Mom got a full-time job at the university, teaching English literature, and she was hoping to get tenure in a couple of years. As far as I can understand, tenure basically means you have a job for life. Dad found lots of work in construction.

Two years later, my mom got pregnant. According to my mom, my dad would talk to me every night and I would "answer" with little kicks.

When she was seven months pregnant, Mom got a call from Dad's foreman. Dad had collapsed on the job. Just like that – keeled over. He was taken away by an ambulance. Mom drove as fast as she could to the hospital, but by the time she got there, he was DOA.

Dead on Arrival.

Apparently he was already dead on departure too . . . dead when he hit the ground. All that time, my dad had had an aneurism (*seminar, surname, armies, marines, manure, remains*) in his brain, a little blood vessel that had been slowly swelling like a balloon. That day it just burst.

So I never met my dad, or any of his side of the family for that matter. His parents died when he was young. He had an older brother back in Australia, but I guess he and my mom lost touch because we never hear from him.

I have lots of pictures of my dad, almost all of them taken by my mom. Mom will talk about him, but only when I ask. Nana Ruth will talk to me about him too, but since we moved to Edmonton, Alberta, when I was two; then to Regina, Saskatchewan, when I was five; then to Kelowna, BC, when I was nine; then to Vancouver this summer, right after I turned twelve, I have only seen her a handful of times. She has come to visit us, but, at most, once a year because she doesn't like to fly.

Last time Nana Ruth visited, we were still in Kelowna, where Mom was a sessional lecturer at UBC Okanagan. I heard them arguing on her last night there.

"Irene, enough is enough," Nana Ruth said. "You have got to move on with your life and stop living in the past." Then Mom told her she *was* moving on with her life, that she was doing the best she could, and she was sick of Nana judging her all the time.

So, I don't know. Maybe that's another reason why Nana Ruth doesn't visit anymore.

From little things I have heard and little clues I have picked up, I suspect my mom was quite a different person when Dad was alive. But I have only ever known her ADD – After Dad's Death. This is the only version of her I'm acquainted with, and it's a version that I love very much.

I also know that she loves me like crazy. So I can't really imagine what it must have been like for her when she got the phone call this time. Because hearing "Your son is in hospital" must have sounded a lot like "Your husband is in hospital."

And we all know how that turned out.

— 4 —

E R A B M S O

somber, bream, sober, bare, bear, bore, robes, smear, some

A M B R O S E

hat's how I got my name. Ambrose. It was my dad's name. It comes from the Greek "Ambrotos" and means "divine, immortal one."

I pointed out the irony of that to my mother once. I said, "Kind of funny, isn't it, seeing as Dad clearly wasn't. Immortal, that is."

Mom didn't think it was funny at all.

P X S D E O E

pox, dope, pod, deep, sex, pee, does, do, posed

EXPOSED

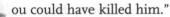

"Y ou could have killed him."

My mom's voice was calm, but in a creepy, just-barely kind of way. She was wearing her best suit, the navy blue one that she'd bought at Goodwill when we lived in Regina. It had gold buttons on the jacket and made her look classy and businesslike all at once. I sat beside her in a straight-backed chair, and because I'd wanted to look businesslike too, I'd worn my brown pants (which were a little tight in the crotch) and a blue-and-white striped button-up shirt that I'd found at Value Village. It was two sizes too big, but it still looked good.

Troy, Mike, and Josh sat opposite us, all squished together on the principal's couch, which was old and plaid and gave off a funny smell. They hadn't made any effort to dress up. In between us, at his desk, sat our principal, Mr. Acheson. He had the look of a guy who'd been a jock in his day, but now he was kind of flabby and almost bald. He was wearing one of his famous ties (the one with the dancing frogs). I think he hoped the ties would make the kids like him better.

They didn't.

I'd been released from hospital the day before. Other than still feeling a bit shaky, I was physically okay. But mentally, I was a wreck.

"It was supposed to be a joke," said Troy, gazing at me with his tiny eyes like he wanted to squash me.

My mom stiffened. "A joke. So, your idea of humor is to risk a friend's life."

"It was an accident," Mike interjected, but Mom just stared daggers at him.

"An *accident?*" Her voice was rising. "You three deliberately put a peanut in my son's sandwich, knowing that he had a deadly peanut allergy. What kind of heartless half-wits –"

"Please, Ms. Bukowski, calm down," the principal said.

"*Mrs.* Bukowski," Mom replied. "And calm down? My son was almost killed and you're asking me to f—ing calm down?"

Oh, man. I'd been keeping my fingers crossed that Mom wouldn't get to the foulmouthed trucker stage.

"I could file criminal charges against these three punks: assault causing bodily harm, willful malice –"

"Ms. Bukowski," the principal said firmly.

"*Mrs.* Bukowski."

"If you're going to make threats like that, I'll have to call the boys' parents as well as the school board superintendent."

Mom actually shut up. There was an uneasy silence for a moment.

"Boys, what do you have to say for yourselves?" asked Mr. Acheson.

"We thought he was exaggerating," Josh said.

"Yeah, how could we know he was serious?" Mike added.

"Because he's your friend!" Mom shouted.

Troy snorted. I sank a little further into my seat.

Mom stared at him. "What was that?"

"Nothing," Troy mumbled.

"No, I'd like to know."

"He's not our friend," Troy said.

Mom shook her head. "If he's not your friend, then why did you invite him to your birthday party?"

Like I said. Poop. Fan. *Kapooey.*

Troy blinked, confused. "My birthday's not till March."

Mom looked at me, but I pretended I'd just found something really interesting on my Ikes.

"See? He's a big fat liar," Mike said.

"Now, boys –" Mr. Acheson began.

"He told us his family was loaded and the only reason he went to a public school was because his parents wanted him to mix with regular kids," said Troy.

"He told us you spent your weekends up at Whistler, in your chalet," Josh added.

Mike said, "But it didn't make sense, the way he dresses and all. . . ."

"Flood pants and fake Nikes."

"Yeah, if he has so much money, why does he walk around with a hot pink fanny pack?"

Okay, so I'd experimented with the truth. But being honest about myself hadn't exactly worked for me at my other schools, so I'd decided to try something new this time.

"We thought the peanut thing was another lie," said Troy. "You know, another way of trying to get our attention. We wanted to make a point, I guess."

My mom was speechless. I could feel her looking at

me, but I kept staring at my shoes, like I was willing an N to appear.

Mr. Acheson finally filled the silence. "Ms. . . . Mrs. . . . Bukowski. This was a terribly unfortunate event, and we are deeply sorry for the pain it's caused. The boys have each received a severe reprimand and their parents have been informed. They're also on lunchroom cleanup for a month. They know that if anything like this, or even close to this, ever happens again, they will be suspended. But after hearing what the boys have to say, I don't see what more we can do."

I waited for the next round of swears to come spewing out of my mom's mouth. But instead, she just stood up. "Thank you for your time," she said, brushing a strand of hair off her face.

Then she walked out.

Without me.

I sat there for a moment, not sure what to do. Finally I said, "No hard feelings on my part, dudes." I aimed for a casual smile, but they stared at me like I was a total idiot. Even Mr. Acheson looked embarrassed for me.

So I stood up, deciding I could at least walk out with my head held high, but I guess my leg had fallen asleep because it gave out from under me and I almost fell. I caught myself on the edge of Mr. Acheson's desk, spilling his pencil holder. I started to gather up the pencils, but he said – rather sharply, I thought – "Just leave it."

So I walked out of the office, dragging my sleeping leg behind me. And feeling like the biggest loser in the world.

— 6 —

P H A U P Y N

nap, nappy, pun, puny, up, ha, pan, pay, hay

U N H A P P Y

I had to practically run to keep up with my mother as we headed back to our place, which wasn't easy because my leg was still numb. Fortunately, we lived only three blocks from the school, so it didn't take long to get to our house.

Well, our basement. We rent the basement suite in a house in Kitsilano, a neighborhood on the west side of Vancouver, right on the bus route to Mom's work.

We moved here for my mom's new job. She's what's called a sessional lecturer at the University of British

Columbia. It means she teaches a bunch of courses on contract, but she's not really an employee. It's the same job she's had in all the other places we've lived. Every time she hopes she'll be hired on full-time, and every time it doesn't happen.

I like our new neighborhood. We're on West 7th Ave., a two-minute walk to all the shops on Broadway and a twenty-minute walk to Jericho Beach, one of the most beautiful parks I've ever seen. We walked down there the day after we moved here, and it was the first time I'd ever set eyes on the Pacific Ocean, or any ocean, come to think of it.

The house we live in is owned by Mr. and Mrs. Economopoulos, a friendly Greek couple who live upstairs. They didn't call our place a basement in the ad; they called it a "garden suite." Mom kind of took them to task for that when we looked at the place, but they still rented it to us. Actually (and without meaning to brag), I think they rented it to us because of me. Mrs. Economopoulos, who is plump and smells like fresh-baked bread and wears shapeless dresses with flesh-colored nylons that stop at the knee, pinched my cheeks a lot that day and kept saying I reminded her of her youngest son, Cosmo, when he was my age.

"He was beautiful boy," she said. Then her eyes filled with tears and she pinched my cheeks again and she told my mom she could have the place if she wanted it and she would even knock fifty bucks off the rent.

I like their house. It's white stucco and surrounded by a low, wrought-iron fence. The front yard has a bird-bath in the middle of a big flower garden, which Mrs. E says will be full of roses in the spring. The backyard is even bigger, and a third of it is full of Mr. E's tomato plants, protected by a huge plastic tarp. They also have a big deck off the kitchen, where Mr. E barbecues in all kinds of weather.

The door to our place is at the side of the house, and we have our own sidewalk to lead us there.

Our basement suite isn't as big as our place was in Kelowna, or as sunny as our place in Regina, but, as Mom points out, rents were cheaper there so we could get more for our money. It's got two bedrooms, a com-bination living-room/kitchen, and a big bathroom. Mom has covered the living room walls with her photo-graphs. She used to be quite into photography when Dad was alive, and her pictures, mostly of trees and flowers and beaches, have made all of our apartments feel more like home.

All in all, it's a fine place, and so far it's only flooded once. When that happened, the Economopouloses were really nice about getting it cleaned up for us, and we even spent a couple of nights in their spare bedroom. This was fun because, on the first night, Mrs. Economopoulos made us an enormous Greek dinner, with souvlaki and moussaka and even that cheese that you light on fire. And once Mom had made her swear on her statuette of the Virgin Mary that there were no peanuts in anything, I was allowed to stuff my face. Man, was it delicious, and no offense to my mother, but Mrs. E is a way better cook. Mr. and Mrs. E told us a lot of stories about growing up in Greece and about the bakery they used to run, until they both retired last year. Mrs. E translated for Mr. E, who still doesn't speak much English even though he's lived here for over thirty years. It was really fun. As weird as it sounds, it almost felt more like home than home.

The only not-so-nice part in the evening was when the grown-ups were drinking coffee in the living room after supper. Mr. E sat in his favorite chair, a big leather La-Z-Boy. Mrs. E and I sat on the couch, which had a clear plastic cover on it and made fart sounds every time anyone moved. Mom was standing up and studying a wall full of framed photos of their kids. "You have three children?" she asked.

"Yes. Vivian, she's the eldest, she's twenty-eight, married to a doctor," Mrs. E said, beaming with pride, then pointed at her feet. "Podiatrist. He makes a lot of money doing the feet. Nick, he's the middle child, he's twenty-six and working very hard selling cars. He's a very good boy."

"BMW and Lexus," Mr. E added.

There was silence for a moment, then Mom asked, "And your youngest?"

"Cosmo," said Mrs. E, and suddenly her eyes were filled with tears like they were on the day she pinched my cheeks, and Mr. E started talking loudly in Greek.

"I'm sorry," my mom said. "I didn't mean to upset you."

"Is he dead?" I asked, and Mom gave me the stink-eye, which didn't seem fair because I knew that the question had been on the tip of her tongue.

"No," said Mrs. E. "He's in jail."

Then Mr. E shouted at Mrs. E in Greek and he stormed out of the room.

"My husband, he's mad, I tell you. He thinks you'll think we're bad people because of Cosmo."

"Goodness, of course not," my mom said, but in a phony kind of way.

"Why's he in jail?" I asked.

From the look on my mom's face, you'd think I'd just asked what color underwear Mrs. E was wearing. Mrs. E started to cry, and Mom gave me the stink-eye again and said, "Ambrose, that's none of our business." But give me a break. I knew she was dying to know, too.

Anyway, everyone calmed down after a while and we all had seconds of dessert. Then we watched "The Amazing Race," one of Mr. E's favorite shows. Mom had tried to get us to go to our room before it came on, but I just ate my dessert really, really slowly because I'd heard kids talk about this show but had never seen it (despite the fact that it had been on for years). It was great – I was on the edge of my seat from beginning to end. Even my mom, who won't let us get cable because she says TV is a mindless waste of time, got sucked into the drama of it all. Mr. E spent the whole time shouting at the contestants in Greek.

Afterward, we went to bed. They gave us Vivian's old room, which had twin beds. A huge collection of Barbie dolls lined the shelves.

I asked my mom again, "Why do you think their son's in jail?"

"I have no idea."

We lay in the dark for a few minutes, then I asked, "What if he's a murderer and he escapes and comes home for some of his mom's cooking? Which was amazing, by the way." I burped and got a taste of moussaka in my mouth, mingled with toothpaste, which wasn't as bad as it sounds.

All I got in response was a gentle snore.

When we arrived home from the meeting at school, the Economopouloses were out on their porch.

"Hi, Irene; hi, Ambrose."

"Hi, Mr. and Mrs. E," I said.

Mom just waved and kept walking to our door. Over the years I'd noticed that she didn't get too friendly with our landlords. When we entered, she still didn't say anything. She just opened a bottle of wine and started getting dinner ready, so I went to my room.

My room faces the garden, so through my high-up window I can see the grass, and if I stand on my bed, I can see Mr. E's tomato plants. I have glow-in-the-dark stars all over my ceiling, which I'm now starting to think might be kind of babyish, but I still like gazing up at them after I've turned off my light. Definitely babyish is my bedspread, which is covered in Buzz Lightyear images from *Toy Story*, but Mom says we can't afford another one for a while. There's a small white-painted desk in the corner, loaned to us by the Economopouloses. Two big mason jars sit on the desk. One is filled with bottle caps, which I collect. I've managed to find some really unique ones, maybe because I'm always looking at the ground when I walk. The other jar is filled over halfway with quarters. I've been saving quarters since I was little, and whenever the jar fills up, my mom and I put the money into a special bank account for my university education.

I don't have a door, but Mom and I bought these cool multicolored plastic beads that hang from the frame and make a clickity sound every time I walk in or out.

I have a big poster of the moon above my bed and one of the human body on the opposite wall. My only other picture sits beside my bed in a frame. It's one of my dad, taken by my mom only a few months before he died. He's looking right at me, and his eyes are all crinkled and he has this huge grin on his face. Mom said she'd just told him a joke, but whenever I ask what the joke was, she says she can't remember.

He was really handsome, my dad. He had thick brown hair and tanned skin and muscles, and he was so tall – six feet, three inches – a full foot taller than my mom. She told me once that he used to call her Squirt, but when I tried calling her that, she asked me not to.

Sometimes I stare at myself in the bathroom mirror, trying to see if any part of me looks like him. But I just can't imagine that my dad was ever short or scrawny or bowlegged, or that his hair had a cowlick at the front, or that his nose was too big for his face. Lookswise, I must have got some sort of recessive gene.

Anyway, I gave the picture of my dad a quick wave, which I always do when I enter my room. It may sound dorky, but I know deep down in my gut that he sees me waving and that he wishes he could be here to watch me grow up, play ball with me, and talk to me about girls and puberty and embarrassing erections (*entices, esoteric, notices, cistern, corniest*), of which I have now had at least a dozen. Thank God for textbooks that a guy can

34

put in front of his pants if he needs to walk across a room. And I'm not even going to start about wet dreams.

But even if Dad can't be here physically, I think he's watching over us.

And I know he loves Mom. And I know he loves me.

After supper, I washed the dishes while Mom drank her third glass of wine and paid some bills. I could hear her talking to herself and swearing a little. Bills always make her do that.

She still hadn't said anything about the meeting at school. When we were both done, she pulled out the Scrabble board, which was a good sign because she was sticking to our routine.

There's not a lot I'm good at. I'm good at school, but not exceptional. I'm lousy at sports. My mom once scrimped and saved so I could take trombone lessons. I was so hopeless, we gave it up after three months.

But I'm good at Scrabble. In fact, my mom calls me a Scrabble genius because I beat her all the time. She finds this mostly amusing, but also a little irritating. "And to think I'm the one with the Ph.D. in English lit," she'll say.

Tonight was no exception. I laid down the words "LEGUME," "ZIP" (on a triple word score), and "MEMENTO," in front of an "S," which got me a bonus

35

of fifty points for using all my letters. But my favorite part in the game was at the very beginning. I had to go first, and I had a terrible rack of letters: "HPYKIOT." I stared at them for a long time, moving the tiles around, and just as my mom was starting to get restless and drum her fingertips on the table (which was really annoying and actually against our family rules), suddenly I saw it: "PITHY." I laid it down on the double word star in the middle for twenty-six points.

Later, when we were putting away the board, Mom said, "What did you do with the book?"

"What book?"

"The book we bought for Troy's birthday party. *The Thief Lord.*"

Oh. That book. "I left it at Planet Lazer."

She nodded. "And what did you do there for three hours?"

"I read the book in the bathroom. It was very good."

She put the Scrabble game back on the shelf and poured the last of the wine into her glass.

"I'm sorry, Mom. I don't know why I lied. It's just . . . starting at another new school, it's not easy, and I thought if I made it seem like I was someone . . . someone, I don't know –"

"Someone else?"

I didn't answer.

Mom picked up her wineglass. "I think I'll go to bed and read," she said.

"Okay," I replied. But I knew this conversation wasn't over.

And I was right.

E H O D B E A N

honed, bane, done, heed, debone, need, dean, hen

B O N E H E A D

n Sunday, we walked all the way to Granville Island along the waterfront. It was overcast, but it wasn't raining.

I like Granville Island, even though technically it isn't an island at all since a road runs right to it. It's a happy place. Mom and I bought apples fresh from the Okanagan at the market and some pizza buns from our favorite bakery. We ate them by the water's edge while we watched the aquabuses – funny-looking little boats that take foot passengers across False Creek to downtown.

That's when the conversation started up again.

"You don't seem to have much luck in the regular school system," Mom said.

"Gee, thanks."

"It's not a criticism. Just an observation. A lot of famous people didn't do well in the regular school system."

"Oh, yeah? Like who?"

"Like the Brontë sisters." I rolled my eyes. Only my mom would call the Brontë sisters famous.

"And Einstein," she continued. "He had to stand in the corner with a dunce cap on his head."

"You're making that up."

She smiled. "And Nelson Mandela got the strap every week. And Gandhi got lots of detentions."

Now, I was laughing. I fed a bit of my bun to a bunch of squawking seagulls.

"I met with Principal Acheson yesterday," she said.

"You did? When?"

"When you were helping Mr. Economopoulos clean out his garage." I helped Mr. E on the weekends sometimes, cutting his grass with a push mower or doing other odd jobs for a bit of pocket money. "We talked through the options, and he suggested correspondence schooling."

"Correspondence schooling? What's that?"

"Basically, you get all of your work from the district correspondence school and you do the work at home."

"With no one to teach me?"

"Well, I would supervise you. And you'd have a teacher you could access on-line."

"But we don't have a computer." Mom doesn't believe in computers, especially in the Internet. She says it's a haven for pornographers and pedophiles. But that's a bit hypocritical if you ask me, because she has access to a computer at the university any time she wants.

"Mr. Acheson says that he can arrange to get you some computer time since Cypress is a community access school. I'll have to be with you because if you're not a student at the school, they can't let you be on your own. Liability issues, apparently."

"How can you do that? You teach during the day."

"The department needs a sessional to teach in the evenings, too. Five nights a week, from six to ten. I talked to the dean, and he says I can make the switch."

"And you'll leave me home alone?"

"I'm not thrilled about that part. We'll have to have some rules, and I'm going to ask Mrs. Economopoulos to keep an eye on you." Her voice cracked a little, and I looked at her and saw that she was trying not to cry.

"Mom, don't . . . I'll go back to Cypress, seriously. I don't want to mess things up for you."

"Oh, Ambrose," she said, and pulled me close. "You don't mess things up for me. Don't ever think that." She blew her nose on an old Kleenex she'd found in the pocket of her jeans. "So what do you say? Shall we give correspondence school a try?"

"I guess," I said. And as we sat there watching the boats on the water, I started to make a mental list of the pros and cons:

THE PROS
a) no more Three Stooges
b) no more fag jokes
c) no more impatient teachers who get annoyed when I ask too many questions, or when I squeal because the Three Stooges have flushed my lunch down the toilet
d) no more schedules
e) no more gym class, where they make you change into dorky shorts in front of all the other guys (one day I forgot to wear underwear and it was the worst day of my life, even worse than the day I almost died)

THE CONS

a) no more sneaking peeks at Ms. Martin's boobs
   in music class when she props them up on top
   of her guitar and they're big and they move a
   little and you can see the edge of her bra (but
   this one is also a pro because I once got a boner
   watching those boobs and had to sit with
   my sheet music over my lap for the rest of
   the lesson).

That was the only con I could come up with. I felt a
little flutter of excitement in my stomach.

Correspondence school was going to be great.

— 8 —

E I U P S R R S

super, purse, press, spur, pure, ruse, user, uprise

S U R P R I S E

As November began, so did the rain. The days were shorter too, and because we were in a basement it sometimes felt like we were living in a cave, even in the middle of the day. I didn't mind so much, but it bothered my mom. At first, as a treat, we'd put on all the lights when we woke up in the morning and keep them on, but it wasn't environmentally friendly and it made Mom choke when she got the Hydro bill, so we had to stop.

By the middle of the month, we'd settled into our new routine. Because Mom now worked till ten and didn't get home till almost eleven, our days started later than they used to. We'd both sleep till eight-thirty, then, without bothering to get out of our pajamas, we'd eat our breakfast of no-name cereal and fruit, and Mom would have two mugs of coffee and read the Economopouloses' *Vancouver Sun* newspaper from the day before (they always left it by our door when they were through with it). Around ten o'clock, we'd review the work that I needed to do that day (which was sent by the district correspondence school), then Mom would make me shower and get dressed and I'd get started on my work by ten-thirty.

I could get through my work surprisingly quickly. Take away the classroom setting and a teacher who had thirty other kids to manage, and suddenly stuff that filled a six-hour school day took me two to three hours. While I did my work, Mom would mark papers, grumbling at the students' poor spelling or lack of critical thinking.

"I teach the ones who don't want to be there," she'd tell me, even though she'd told me this a million times before, in every place we'd lived. "Like the engineering students who have to pass one English course, or the ESL students. The tenured professors get to teach the ones who've actually chosen to be there. They dole out the crappy courses to sessionals, like me."

After my schoolwork and her marking were done,

we'd go out for some exercise. Usually this meant a long walk along the beach. Once in a while, we'd go ice-skating at the Kitsilano Community Centre, but I didn't like that so much because Mom insisted that I wear one of their rental helmets, and since she was also worried I'd get head lice from the last person to rent the helmet, I had to wear a toque and then the helmet and it was uncomfortable, not to mention dorky.

On Thursday afternoons at two o'clock, we'd walk over to Cypress Elementary together so I could use a terminal in the computer lab. The first time, I had butterflies in my stomach – more like elephants, really, because I did not want to run into the Three Stooges. But it was good timing. All the kids were in class, and the lab was empty. Two weeks in a row, Mr. Acheson dropped by to see how I was doing.

"Your mom sure works hard on your behalf," he said to me one day, with my mom standing right there. I found this kind of annoying. It was like he thought I had special needs or something and needed an advocate. But my mom didn't seem to mind, even when he put one of his beefy paws on her tiny shoulder and gave it a squeeze.

Every weekday at five, Mom had to leave for work. Her new schedule meant we couldn't have our nightly Scrabble games, but sometimes we'd squeeze one in before she left.

She had a list of rules that I was supposed to follow, and she even gave me a cell phone so I could call her no matter where I was (which, according to the rules, could be no further than our local library, four blocks from our house).

At first I enjoyed these evenings to myself. I was my own boss. Mom said I was limited to an hour of TV a night, but she wasn't there to monitor me so I watched as much as I wanted. But since our TV got only one channel, that thrill didn't last too long.

For a while I found other things to do, like eating what I wanted, when I wanted; but Mom didn't buy junk food, or any food that said MAY CONTAIN TRACES OF NUTS, and, to be honest, eating half a loaf of spelt bread in one sitting didn't exactly make my heart race.

One night I wandered eight blocks from our house, a full four blocks farther than I was allowed. Another night I tried some of my mom's wine from an open bottle in the fridge, but it tasted gross.

I was supposed to go to bed at nine-thirty and read, with lights-out by ten, but that was hard because I wasn't used to falling asleep without my mom there. And I guess you could say that I also needed to know she was safe. So most nights I'd wait till I heard her come up the walk, then I'd flip off my light and pretend to be asleep.

By Thursday night of the third week, the novelty was

wearing off and I was pretty bored. I'd already snooped through my mom's drawers, which didn't provide any interesting discoveries and left me feeling kind of yucky. It was pouring rain outside and the wind had picked up, and once in a while the window frames rattled, making me think that someone was trying to break in. I turned on the TV for company and watched David Suzuki's "The Nature of Things," while eating a rubbery piece of my mom's "famous breaded chicken." I was trying to convince myself that there was no escaped psycho killer on the loose, when there was a knock on the door. I almost leapt out of my skin. For a moment I sat silent because Mom had made me promise not to open the door, in case a pedophile was waiting on the other side. But since I could clearly see Mrs. Economopoulos's stout figure through the gauze curtain that hung on the window right beside the door, I decided to live life on the edge. I got up and opened it.

Mrs. E held out a plate of baklava. "No peanuts," she said.

"Thanks!" I said, and I meant it. Her baklava was like biting into a crisp yet moist piece of heaven.

"Your mama's at work?"

I nodded. She gazed at my plate of food. "You make that? It looks terrible."

I figured I shouldn't rat out my mom, so I just said, "It tastes terrible, too."

Mrs. E took the plate out of my hand and set it on the table beside the baklava. "You're eating with us. I made moussaka."

Who was I to argue? I dumped the rest of my chicken into the garbage, being careful to cover it with other, older garbage so Mom wouldn't see it. Then I followed Mrs. E upstairs.

"Mrs. E, you're the best cook ever," I said, as I settled onto their plastic-covered couch to watch "The Amazing Race" with Mr. E after supper.

Mrs. E pinched my cheeks and handed me another honey cookie before she headed back to the kitchen to do the dishes.

I was belching under my breath and watching the recap from last week's show when the doorbell rang. Mr. E looked very comfortable in his La-Z-Boy, so I offered to answer it.

"If they want money, you slam the door," said Mr. E, as I walked out of the room.

But the guy at the door didn't look like he was going to ask for money. He was twenty-five or so, average height, with muscles bulging out from under his tight black T-shirt. His dark brown hair was cropped short, almost like an army buzz cut, and he had a tattoo of a laughing skull on his right bicep. He was holding a duffel bag, and I was thinking of telling Mr. E to call 911 when the guy spoke.

"Who the hell are you?"

That wasn't any of his business, so I just said, "Who the hell are you?"

"Who is it, Ambrose?" shouted Mrs. E, as she approached from the kitchen. She was carrying a plate, and when she saw who was at the door, she dropped it. It smashed into a bunch of pieces on the floor.

The crash was followed by a high-pitched scream, and I hoped Mr. E was calling the cops because Mrs. E launched herself at the guy. I thought she was going to hit him, but instead she threw her arms around him and hugged him tight.

"Cosmo! My baby! My baby is home!"

9

L I C I R M A N

claim, mail, rain, rail, nail, lima, ra, car, mini, lira

C R I M I N A L

Mom was surprised to find me waiting up for her on the couch when she got home.

"Ambrose, how come you're not in bed? Is everything okay?"

"He came back."

"Who came back?"

"Cosmo. Mr. and Mrs. E's jailbird son."

I'd been listening to my mom's CD's on our boom box for almost two hours, dying to tell her the news. "I was up there having dinner, they invited me, and he just showed up on the doorstep," I told her, "and asked me who the hell I was. And then Mrs. E screamed and then she hugged him and then she started hitting him –"

"*Whoa*, slow down. Are you alright?"

Was I alright? Sometimes Mom could totally miss the point.

"I'm fine. He just stood there and let his mom hit him, then Mr. E came out and boy, did he give Cosmo the stink-eye. Then he told me I had to go home, so I didn't even get to see what team got booted off 'The Amazing Race.' And I came down here, but I could hear them shouting and Mrs. E crying, for, like, a long time."

My mom sank into a chair and took off her shoes.

"And he totally looks the part of an ex-con, too. Like a thug. Big muscles, tattoo, buzz cut – they probably gave him that haircut in prison. And I still don't know why he was in jail, but I'll find out –"

"No, you won't."

"Yeah, next time I'm over –"

"You're not going over there anymore. Not without me. Do you understand?"

And suddenly I realized my humongous error. I was talking to Mom like she would get how cool this all was, forgetting that I was talking to *Mom*.

"Mom, come on –"

"I'm serious, Ambrose. We have no idea what that young man did, and I don't want you anywhere near him."

"But, Mom, Mrs. E's a great cook. And the finale of 'The Amazing Race' is next week."

"My decision is final."

She walked into her room and closed her door. And I knew there was no point even trying to argue. Because "my decision is final" was really code for "I couldn't keep your dad safe. And I won't make the same mistake with you."

But, of course, telling me to stay away from Cosmo was like telling a little kid not to lick a metal fence post in the middle of winter. Suddenly all you can think about is putting your tongue against the metal post. *What will happen? What will it taste like? Will your whole tongue really come off when you pull?* It becomes an obsession, and I know this from personal experience.

Besides, staying away from Cosmo required effort. The guy lived right upstairs.

Four days later, my mom had just left for work and I was settling in at our kitchen table to do my math when I heard a car pull up – a very noisy car that didn't sound at all like the Economopouloses' Ford Escort. I dropped my pencil and hurried outside to see a beat-up red sports car in the driveway. Cosmo climbed out of the driver's seat, wearing faded jeans and a leather jacket.

"I think you need a new muffler," I told him, trying to help.

Cosmo just glared at me and walked into the garage. I was about to head back inside when he appeared again, carrying a bucket and a sponge. He found the hose at the side of the house and started filling the bucket with water.

"Gonna wash the car?"

"Good guess, Einstein."

"What kind of car is it?"

"'91 Camaro. Friend of mine let me keep it in his garage while I was away."

"You mean, while you were in jail."

This earned me another glare. He pulled a pack of cigarettes from his pocket and lit one.

"That's bad for you," I said.

He didn't comment, but just started washing the car. I stood and watched. I don't mind watching people go about their business, but I've found that sometimes they mind me watching them.

"You're giving me the creeps," Cosmo said, after a while.

"Why?"

"Don't you have somewhere you need to be?"

"No."

He looked at me like I was an alien. "Those are very interesting pants."

"Thanks." I was wearing my favorite purple cords. "I could help you," I added.

"Don't need it, thanks." He took a long drag off his cigarette.

"Have you ever stopped to think about the names they give cars? Like *Neon*. Who wants to drive a Neon? Or *Aspire*. Aspire to what – owning a better car?"

I laughed at my own joke, but he didn't crack a smile. He just took off his leather jacket to rinse the soap off his car, the cigarette dangling from his mouth. I could see his tattoo move as he worked.

"What did you do?" I asked.

He glanced up at me, squinting in the sun.

"Why did they throw you in the slammer?"

Cosmo raised an eyebrow. "The slammer?"

I nodded. "Should I be worried for my personal safety?"

He studied me for a second. Then he lowered his voice: "You really want to know?"

I nodded again, even though an icy finger of fear was working its way up my back.

He glanced around to make sure no one was listening. "I got sent away for killing a boy just about your age. A boy who asked too many stupid questions. One day, I just snapped."

Then, with one swift motion, he grabbed something and pointed it at me, and I thought I was going to poo in my pants. I ducked, but it was too late. I was hit –

With water. From the hose. Within seconds I was soaked.

After I'd changed out of my wet clothes and hidden them under my bed so Mom wouldn't ask questions, I went straight back to my math homework. But it was hard to concentrate. I was pretty sure he'd been pulling my leg about murdering the kid. But not so sure that I didn't barricade our door with a chair first. Just to be on the safe side.

10

U R R E D M R E

re, red, mud, drum, rude, reed, deer, me

M U R D E R E R

"*lech,* I'm drenched," said my mom. It was Saturday and we had just come home from buying fruits and vegetables on Broadway at the Golden Valley, where the woman who runs the place always tries to give me a free candy but Mom always refuses. We'd been caught in a rainstorm on the way home, and Mom got the worst of it because she wasn't wearing her rain jacket.

When she went into the bedroom to get changed

and I started putting away our groceries, there was a tap at the door.

"Can you get that?" Mom called.

Now I was still pretty sure Cosmo had been pulling my leg about killing a kid, but as a guy can never be too careful, I grabbed the closest weapon – a mesh bag full of oranges – and quietly approached the door, asking myself if I really thought I could thwart a killer, armed with citrus fruit.

I couldn't see anyone through the gauze curtain of our window. "Who is it?" I said, in a deep voice.

"Soula." It took me a moment to remember that Soula was Mrs. Economopoulos's first name. I put down the oranges and threw open the door. "My brother has slaughtered a lamb," she said. "He gave us half. We'd like to have you to dinner tonight."

Mom and I hardly ever ate red meat. Mom had "moral issues," and besides, it was beyond our budget. I, on the other hand, loved red meat. My body craved it. *But what if Cosmo had been telling the truth? What if he snapped again and made me his next victim during dinner? Was it really worth risking my life for a few helpings of lamb?*

The answer was obvious. "We'd love to," I said quickly, before my mom could dream up an excuse. She'd just come out of her room and I could tell from the look on her face that she was thinking hard to come up with one.

"But, Ambrose, don't we have –"

"Nope. We have nothing planned. Nothing."

Mrs. E smiled. "Great. Come at five-thirty." Her smile wavered slightly as she added, "You'll get a chance to meet Cosmo. He's really a good boy."

Despite being a killer, I thought, as Mrs. E left the apartment – even though I didn't really believe him.

But when we arrived for dinner, Cosmo was nowhere to be seen. Mom handed over a jar of her homemade apple chutney, which I secretly called upchuck-ney because it tasted awful.

We made small talk for a while in their living room and I admired their plate and spoon collections, which hung on one wall. They'd put on their gas fireplace and it was bright and cheerful, despite the continuing rain outside. Mr. E poured Mom a glass of their homemade wine. I got a glass of Coke, and I was grateful that my mom didn't launch into her speech about pop having no nutritional value whatsoever, which would then morph into her speech about the corporatization of the world by companies like Coca Cola Ltd.

When we sat down to eat in the dining room, the table was set for five.

"Is Cosmo joining us?" I asked.

Mr. E shrugged apologetically. "With Cosmo, you never know."

"You must be glad to have him home," my mom said, and I could tell she was going on a fishing expedition.

But all Mr. E said was "Yes, happy."

"He's a good boy," Mrs. E said, for the second time that day.

The food was amazing. Barbecued lamb and roasted potatoes and this special spinach dish that actually made me like spinach. Mom couldn't resist asking if everything was peanut-free. By now, this seemed a bit insulting, but Mrs. E cheerfully reassured her. Mr. and Mrs. E even politely took a spoonful each of mom's chutney and told her it was delicious.

I was admiring the big chandelier that hung over the table when we heard the front door open.

"Cosmo? You want some food?" Mr. E called out.

No one answered. I caught a glimpse of Cosmo's back as he headed down the hall. Mr. and Mrs. E shared a quick, worried glance, and I could tell from my mom's tight smile that she was feeling uneasy. Then

Mr. E picked up the platter full of lamb and asked, "Who wants seconds?"

To which I naturally replied, "Me."

After dinner, Mr. and Mrs. E ushered us back into the living room. Mr. E poured my mom an ouzo (a Greek liqueur that smells like licorice) and gave me another Coke, while Mrs. E brought out a tray of homemade pink and white meringues.

We sat on the crinkly couch and pretty soon the adults got into a big discussion about real estate prices in Vancouver. Mom was complaining that she'd never be able to afford to buy here, which I thought was ironic, and maybe even hypocritical, because the truth was, we couldn't afford to buy anywhere on what she made, and that is not a complaint, just a fact. Mrs. E was saying they'd bought back in the late seventies, when things were more affordable. It was kind of boring, so I drifted. I ate a second meringue, pink this time, and washed it down with Coke. Then I thought about the words you could make from "Economopoulos" (*monocles, compels, compose, clomps, clumps, columns, consume, coupons, pounces*) and had just come up with *couples*, when I suddenly let out an enormous and totally unexpected belch.

"Ambrose!" my mom said.

"I'm sorry. Really. It was the Coke," I said, which made me realize that I really, really needed to pee. But I knew the washroom was down the same hall that Cosmo had disappeared down, and I might run into him. I held it for as long as I could, and I even thought about making a dash for the bathroom at our place, but I couldn't see how to explain that. So, finally, I excused myself and bolted down the corridor, past another spoon collection hanging on the wall and into the washroom.

I locked the door, then I peed for what felt like five minutes straight. I did some other stuff, too, because when you're not used to eating a lot of meat, it sometimes doesn't digest that well.

When I left the washroom, I saw him. He was in his room, at a desktop computer. It looked like he hadn't bothered to redecorate since he was a teenager. The walls were still covered with Guns N' Roses posters and one practically life-size poster of Pamela Anderson, which hung over his bed.

I stared at Pam for a while, which made me feel tingly, then I tried to see what was on his computer screen, but his back was blocking my view. I don't know why, but I wanted to see what he was looking at. Well, I sort of *do* know why: I was hoping he was looking at pictures of naked women, maybe even naked Pamela Anderson. Even though I didn't really believe he'd killed a kid, I figured he wouldn't try to murder me with his parents and my mom down the hall, so I walked into the room.

What I saw on the computer screen was disappointing and surprising all at once. He was in the middle of an online Scrabble game.

"You play Scrabble?"

Cosmo almost jumped out of the chair. "Jesus Christ. Don't sneak up on people like that."

"I play Scrabble, too."

"That's great." But he didn't say it like he meant it. He turned back to his game.

"I'm quite good."

He didn't answer. I could see him staring at his letters: GINWXAQ. Eventually he placed the word "WING," using "ING" from his own letters and attaching them to an existing "W." The "G" was on a double word square, so it got him sixteen points.

"Huh," I said.

"Huh? What does 'huh' mean?"

"Nothing."

"Has anyone ever told you you're annoying?"

"Yes."

"I bet you drive your teachers nuts."

"I don't have any teachers right now."

"What are you talking about?"

"I don't go to school."

He turned away from his screen and looked at me.

62

"What do you mean, you don't go to school? Everyone goes to school."

"I'm homeschooled. Well, correspondence schooled."

"Correspondence schooled. In the middle of Vancouver. Where you're surrounded by schools."

"I used to go to a real school till last month."

"What happened?"

"Three guys tried to kill me."

Cosmo laughed. It was clear he didn't believe me. "Too bad they didn't succeed." He turned back to his game.

"Did you start to play Scrabble in jail?"

"That's none of your business."

"I've played with my mom since I was eight."

"Great. Now look, I really need to concentrate on my next turn."

That's when his opponent laid down "ZOOS," with the "Z" on a triple word score square and the "S" at the end of Cosmo's "WING," getting a total score of fifty-one points.

"Damnit," said Cosmo.

"You should've played 'WAXWING' on your turn instead," I told him. "It's a type of bird. You had all the letters. It would have given you forty-four points instead of sixteen, and you would've blocked your opponent's shot at the triple word score."

Cosmo stared at me.

"You kind of handed him 'ZOOS' on a silver platter," I added.

That's when Cosmo threw his *Official Scrabble Dictionary* at me and I yelled – because it startled me, not because it hurt – and Mom came running into the room. Even though I said everything was fine, she thanked Mr. and Mrs. E for a wonderful evening but said that she had to get me home to bed, which was embarrassing because it was only eight o'clock.

Down in our apartment, I could hear shouting from upstairs, then the front door slamming. Cosmo's Camaro screeched out of the driveway, and I was pretty sure he hadn't finished his Scrabble game.

Which was probably for the best because he was obviously getting slaughtered.

T Y M E P

type, temp, yep, my, yet, met, pet, me, pye

EMPTY

hen I woke up the next morning, I tiptoed out of my room still wearing my rocket-ship pj's, which were starting to ride up my ankles. I thought I'd read my book on the couch for a while and have a piece of toast while Mom slept because she always sleeps late on Sundays.

So I was surprised to see her at the kitchen table, drinking a cup of coffee from the WORLD'S GREATEST MOM mug I'd bought her three years ago at a garage sale for twenty-five cents. She was looking through the

Courier, a free newspaper that got delivered to the door twice a week. I poured a bowl of no-name multigrain flakes into a bowl and chopped up a banana on top and sat beside her. She was looking in the classifieds, under APARTMENTS FOR RENT.

"Mom, c'mon."

"I'm not comfortable living in the same house as that young man," she replied.

"But we don't even know what he did."

"Well, whatever it was, it got him a jail sentence, so it can't be good." She took a sip of her coffee. "I just can't believe how expensive everything is."

We spent the day doing laundry. The Economopouloses had offered their washing machine to my mom a zillion times, but she didn't want to knock on their door and walk through their house to use their machine. So every weekend we wheeled a cartful of dirty clothes up to Broadway and Collingwood to the Laundromat. After laundry, we hit a few garage sales, and Mom found a great cable-knit sweater and I found some old *Spiderman* comics and a kite. Then we walked to Jericho Beach because, for the first time in a while, it was a beautiful day, and we tried to fly the kite. It got tangled up in a tree and we had to leave it there, but at least it had cost only fifty cents.

That night we made a pizza – my favorite – and Mom even let me put pepperoni on half of it. After she'd done a bunch of exam marking, we played Scrabble. I won, 272 to 203, thanks to the words "WHIMSY" on a triple word score and "JIVE" on another, and Mom didn't drink anything but water because the ouzo had made her feel kind of sick the night before. All in all, it was a very nice day.

And then it was Christmas. We bought a little tree. It was very Charlie Brownish, and we decorated it with all the decorations we'd made over the years. We did popcorn strings, and I wound up pricking my thumb with the needle a gazillion times, and we hung home-made paper snowflakes on our door. I liked walking down Broadway from Kidsbooks to Shoppers Drug Mart, where they strung up the most beautiful blue Christmas lights. If I squinted my eyes, the lights would go all fuzzy and it felt the way Christmas should.

On Christmas Day, Mom gave me a multicolored hat with a big pom-pom on top that she'd knit all by herself. And she gave me socks and underwear, and two new books – *Inkheart* by Cornelia Funke and *Bud, Not Buddy* by a guy named Christopher Paul Curtis. Nana Ruth sent me a check for twenty dollars and Mom a check for a hundred.

I gave my mom a picture frame from a kit I'd bought at the craft store on Broadway. I'd decorated it with all sorts of found objects, like moss and dried flowers, and inside I put a photo of the two of us. She got kind of teary-eyed when she opened it.

Then the phone rang and it was Nana Ruth. Mom spoke politely with her for ten minutes or so, then Nana and I talked for over half an hour, getting caught up. It was great to hear her voice. I'd sent her a picture frame too, with the same photo of my mom and me inside. "I love it," she told me. "I've got it sitting right on top of the piano, where I can look at it every day."

"I miss you, Nana."

"I miss you too, Ambrose. What's it like in Vancouver?"

"Not bad. It rains a lot."

"Well, we're having a hailstorm here, so maybe rain is better."

"When will you come and visit?"

There was a pause on the other end of the line. "I'm not sure, hon. Soon, I hope."

After we'd hung up, I felt a little blue. It was very quiet in the house because we were the only people there. The Economopouloses, even Cosmo, had gone to Mr. E's brother's house in Maple Ridge on Christmas Eve, and they were staying until Boxing Day.

We put on Christmas music to fill the silence and ate a late breakfast of pancakes. Afterward we went for a long walk on the beach, then came home and made hot chocolate. For dinner, Mom cooked us a turkey breast because there was no point cooking an entire turkey for just the two of us. She didn't overcook it, like she sometimes did, and it was very good. We had pumpkin pie for dessert and topped it with whipped cream from a can, which was a treat. Then we went for a short walk around the neighborhood to digest our food, and I gazed at all the Christmas lights and peered into all the brightly lit windows, where I could see families and friends enjoying each other's company. When we got home, we watched *It's a Wonderful Life* on the CBC, which we've done every Christmas Day since I can remember. We opened a bottle of champagne – not real champagne because that was too expensive – and Mom even let me have half a glass.

Around eleven o'clock, I went to bed and I waved at the picture of my dad and I wished him a Merry Christmas.

And then I put the pillow over my head so my mom wouldn't hear me and I cried a little because, even though it had been a really nice day, I felt lonelier than I ever had in my entire life.

— 12 —

U E C S E R

cue, sure, ruse, seer, user, us, cure, curse, reuse, secure

RESCUE

By the second week of January, I was back into my correspondence-school routine and bored out of my mind. The initial excitement had worn off. I had no one to talk to all day except my mom, and a cyber-teacher once a week. At nights, when she went to work, I felt lonely in our apartment, but I was under strict orders not to go to the Economopouloses'.

Just before two o'clock on Thursday, my mom and I walked over to Cypress Elementary so I could "talk" to my cyber-teacher on the lab computer. My life had become so dull that this was now the highlight of my week. I wore a big sweater that used to belong to my dad, with a T-shirt underneath so the wool wouldn't itch my skin.

When we walked into the school, the hallways were mercifully deserted. I breathed deeply and took in the smell of books and BO and other kid-smells, and as weird as it sounds, I felt a longing – not to be picked on again, but to be part of something bigger than just me.

Mr. Acheson came by the lab to say hi and ask about our Christmas holiday, which I found kind of weird because the guy never said two words to me the entire time I was at his school, and now he made a point of dropping by to chat every time I showed up.

"How are things going, Ambrose?"

"Fine." He was wearing his Homer Simpson tie today, and the way he stood over me, I could see his nose hairs. Lots of them.

"So far so good with the correspondence school-ing?"

"I guess."

"Irene, is it working out alright for you?"

I waited for my mom to tell him to call her Mrs. Bukowski, but instead she just said, "Yes, Bob, it's going well so far. Thanks for asking."

Bob?

71

"I found some materials about correspondence schooling on the Web that I printed out for you," he said to her, as I logged on to the computer. "Do you have a moment to come to my office?"

I glanced up at Mom, whose face had, for some reason, gone blotchy and red. "Sure. Ambrose, you'll be okay in here?"

"Unless the other computers decide to launch an attack, I should be fine," I said, and I was kind of disappointed that neither of them laughed at my joke.

She and "Bob" left, and I got down to work. It was warm in the lab, so I took off my sweater. I had a lot of questions today, and my cyber-teacher had some comments on an essay I'd handed in the week before on Mesopotamia. By the time I was done, I realized it was almost dismissal time. My mom still hadn't returned. I jogged quickly down the hall to Mr. Acheson's office, but the door was open and they weren't inside.

Then the bell rang. And that's when I realized I'd forgotten my sweater in the lab. It's also when I realized that one of my mom's T-shirts must have wound up in my drawer and that I hadn't even looked at it when I pulled it on because it said NUMBER ONE MOM in huge letters on the front.

I could not be seen. I ran out the front doors of the school and sprinted across the soccer field. But even my Ikes couldn't turn me into a good runner and, within moments, I heard footsteps behind me and they were getting closer. Then a hand grabbed my shoulder and spun me around.

It was Troy.

"Well, if it isn't Spambrose," he said, dropping the soccer ball he'd been holding and taking a few steps toward me.

"Hey, Troy. How's it hanging?"

"Why is it that words that sound normal in someone else's mouth sound so retarded in yours?" said Troy, just as Mike and Josh appeared, flanking him on either side.

"Look at his T-shirt," Mike said, and they all cracked up.

"You really *are* a fag," Josh said, then he made his wrist go limp and pranced around like he figured a homosexual would do.

"I should let you start your game," I said. I tried to step around them, but the three of them blocked my path.

"I was grounded for a month, thanks to you," said Josh.

"I couldn't use my Wii for three weeks," added Troy.

"Well, you guys did almost kill me –"

"It was your fault. If you hadn't been such a frigging liar," Mike said, then he shoved me so hard, I fell to the ground. When I tried to stand up, Troy kicked me and I fell again.

"C'mon, guys, can't we let bygones be bygones?"

"Shut up," said Josh, kicking me hard in the stomach, and even though he was only wearing sneakers, it really hurt. Mike bent down and pulled the Ikes right off my feet and threw them into a garbage can on the edge of the field. Then all three of them were kicking me and it hurt like hell and I started to cry because nothing like this had ever happened to me before . . . well . . . only twice before . . . once in Regina and once in Kelowna, but never this bad. So I tried to curl up in a ball and protect my head, and there was this weird screeching sound, which I realized only later was probably me.

And then suddenly, like the voice of an angel (only not, because it was a harsh, mean voice full of swears), I heard, "Get the f— away from him, you f—ing punks!" And the kicking stopped and I peered up from the ground to see Cosmo striding toward us with his fists at the ready. He looked really scary, and I wasn't the only one who thought so because Troy, Mike, and Josh took off in the other direction as fast as their legs would carry them.

Cosmo helped me up. I was shivering, partly because I was wearing nothing but a T-shirt on a drizzly January day and partly because I was still freaking out.

"You saved my life."

74

"That would be an exaggeration."

I felt my face and my body. I didn't appear to be bleeding, but I was sore all over, especially in the stomach.

"What'd you do to them?"

I shrugged. "They hate me."

Cosmo nodded like this made sense. "You do have a knack for bringing out the worst in people." Then he glanced at my T-shirt. "*Aw* Jesus, kid . . ."

"It was an accident," I said. "I didn't see what it said, I just grabbed it."

I could tell he was trying not to laugh, but a laugh came out anyway. "Where are your shoes?"

I walked over to the garbage can and fished them out.

"Can you get home okay?" he asked, as I put them back on.

I nodded, and then suddenly I was crying again, blubbering and feeling like a giant baby. "I'm sorry," I said. "It just really hurt."

To my surprise, Cosmo stopped laughing. "I bet it did." He put a hand on my shoulder. "C'mon, I'll walk you home."

We took the alley so we wouldn't run into my mom. But as we walked through the back gate I saw her, entering

75

our apartment. "Oh, no," I moaned. "I can't let her see me like this. She'll freak."

Cosmo didn't say a word. He just let me into his place. Mr. and Mrs. E weren't home, so I went into their bathroom and cleaned up, washing off the grime from my scraped-up elbows and my face. Cosmo even went back to the school and grabbed my sweater, when I told him it was missing, so I could put it back on over the T-shirt and my mom would never know the difference. I didn't tell him it had belonged to my dad and that if I'd lost it, I would have hated myself for the rest of my life.

When I came out of the bathroom, Cosmo was in the living room, watching TSN. "Thanks again," I told him.

He stared at the TV. "You should learn how to protect yourself."

I didn't know what to say. *How was I supposed to learn how to protect myself?* It wasn't like Mom could afford to give me karate lessons, or boxing lessons, or any lessons at all, and even if she could, she'd never let me anyway for fear I'd get hurt, which, I guess you could say, was kind of ironic.

But all I said to Cosmo was "Yeah."

I got down to our place just in time to say bye to my mom before she left for the university. She'd been getting worried about me. I told her I'd gone looking for her and she told me she'd gone looking for me, and we agreed we must've just missed each other.

It wasn't till later that I realized I hadn't felt scared of Cosmo at all. I didn't for a moment think he was going to kill me while I was alone with him upstairs, and he hadn't tried to do any of the yucky things my mom had warned me about over the years, like a) touch my penis or b) get me to touch his.

In fact, for a criminal, he didn't seem like a bad guy at all.

13

E A I T H M L I U

math, lime, them, lithium, malt, helm, mule, mail

HUMILIATE

"Sunshine!" I shouted the following Monday, when I looked outside my bedroom window. Standing on my bed, I could just see a band of blue sky.

I dashed into my mom's room. She was still sleeping, but I couldn't resist. "Mom, it's sunny out."

She opened her eyes groggily, then smiled. "Well, this I have to see."

We got dressed to go out right after breakfast. Mom said, "Screw marking and schoolwork. We can do it later." It was great to see her in a cheerful mood.

When we stepped outside, both of us blinked like moles coming up from their underground burrows. "Let's walk around the neighborhood and treat ourselves to a hot chocolate when we're done," Mom said.

We had a great walk. I quizzed Mom on her classes at the university. "Best student?" I said.

"Easy. This young woman who's studying mechanical engineering. Annabelle's her name. She's only taking my class because she needs a certain number of humanities courses. But she's very bright, and she has a beautiful way with the English language. . . . I wish she'd reconsider her field of study, but, on the other hand, she'll find it easier to get a real job with an engineering degree than she ever would with an English degree. Just look at me." I glanced at her when she said this, but she was smiling.

"Worst student?"

She laughed. "Also easy. Carl, a math major. I hope he's better with numbers than he is with words . . . the guy can't string a sentence together, let alone a coherent thought. And the most grating part is, he couldn't care less."

"Friends?"

"Friends?"

"Have you made any friends?"

"Oh. Well, yes. Jane. She's another sessional lecturer. We sometimes grab a coffee together between classes." This was good to know, especially since mom was like me when it came to making friends: not very good at it. I was happy she'd made one, even if she'd beat me to it.

After our walk, we stopped at Yoka's – a little coffee shop on Broadway. Mom went inside to get our hot chocolates while I waited outside and soaked up the sun. I checked out the flyers posted on a hydro pole in front of me. Mostly they were ads for rock concerts and political rallies. Except for one.

DO YOU LOVE THE GAME OF SCRABBLE? it read. COME JOIN US AT THE WEST SIDE SCRABBLE CLUB, WEDNESDAY NIGHTS AT 7:00 P.M., AT THE WEST SIDE UNITED CHURCH. There was an address and a phone number. I didn't have a pen, so I glanced around to make sure no one was watching, then I tore the notice off the pole and stuffed it into my pocket.

I waited till Mom had gone to work, then I knocked on the Economopouloses' door. Mrs. E answered.

"How are you doing, Ambrose? We haven't seen much of you lately."

"Is Cosmo home?" I asked.

Mrs. E looked puzzled, but she disappeared down the hallway and I heard her shouting to Cosmo that he had a visitor.

It took a couple of minutes before Cosmo appeared. He was wearing a white undershirt and boxer shorts, and his hair stood up on end. He looked like he'd just woken up.

"What do you want?"

"Are you working nights?"

He looked confused. "No."

"Then why do you look like you just got up? It's five o'clock in the afternoon. Shouldn't you be looking for a job?"

He tried to close the door, but I wedged my body in before he could.

"I guess it's hard to find work with a criminal record, huh?"

He gave me a dirty look. "Next time I see those kids kicking the piss out of you, I think I'll join in."

"You don't mean that," I said. I pulled the flyer out of my pocket and handed it to him.

"Why are you showing me this?"

"I think we should go."

"You think we should go. You and me. To a Scrabble Club."

"It's too far to walk, but I figure you can drive."

He laughed. "You are hilarious. You don't even know it, but you are. You're, like, mildly autistic or something."

"Screw you," I retorted. That was just mean. And, I was pretty sure, untrue. I was *not* autistic (*attics, static,*

81

tacit, acts, tact, cast, cats, cist, cuts, scat, tics). I'd seen
Rain Man.

"Look, no offense, kid, but I'm not joining a bunch
of word nerds."

"Come on, it'll be fun. And it's not like you're too
busy," I added, indicating his boxer shorts and undershirt, which, now that I looked closer, were stained. "If
you don't mind my saying so, you should have a
shower. You kind of smell –"

"Bye, Ambrose."

"Will you think about it?"

"No."

"Please. If you don't go, I can't go either. I need a
drive –"

"*Whoa,* would you look at the knockers on that
chick," he said, staring openmouthed at someone
behind me.

I spun around, looking up and down the street. All I
could see was an older man, walking his bassett hound.

"Where? I don't see –"

The door slammed behind me.

When my mom went to work on Wednesday, she told
me she might be a bit late. "Jane and I are going to have
a drink after work."

"Sure thing," I said.

I read *Bud, Not Buddy* for a while, then forced down some of the chewy tuna casserole Mom had left me. Afterward I put on my rain jacket and my hat, then I walked up to Broadway in the rain, with the rest of the casserole in a yogurt container to give to Preacher Paul. He was a homeless guy who often sat outside the drug store, no matter what the weather. I always said hello to him when Mom and I walked past, even though my mom didn't like me to.

"How's it going, Preacher Paul?" I said tonight.

"Not bad, kid." I don't think he remembered my name, even though I told him every time I saw him, but that was okay.

"You like tuna casserole?"

"Does it have carrots in it?"

"Yeah, but you can pick them out."

He nodded and took the container.

"Sorry I don't have a fork."

"That's okay, the Chinese place will give me chopsticks."

I said good night to Preacher Paul and walked back home. When I was a few houses away, I could see Cosmo in the driveway by his Camaro, talking to someone. As I drew closer, I saw it was a guy a few years older than Cosmo, and tougher looking.

"What? You don't have time to have a drink with your best friend?" the older guy was saying. His voice was like gravel. He had long thinning hair held back by a rubber band and he wore a black leather motorcycle jacket. He was wide and all muscle.

"It's not that, Silvio. I'm just trying to stay on the straight and narrow this time, you know?"

"But it's not as simple as that, is it?" said Silvio, and it came out kind of threatening, not like something a best friend would say. "We left certain things unfinished."

"I know. And I'm working on that. But I don't want to go back there, Sil. . . ."

"That might be out of your hands, buddy. Now, c'mon, one drink."

"I'll meet you for coffee tomorrow."

"Coffee?" Silvio laughed, but you could tell he didn't think it was funny.

"I took the fall that night, Sil. Isn't that enough?"

"Not my fault you went ahead and did the job without me."

"Uncle Cosmo?" That was me talking. The words just popped out of my mouth.

Cosmo and Silvio turned to look at me.

"You ready to take me to Scrabble Club? It starts in half an hour."

Cosmo was so surprised, he didn't answer.

"You got a nephew?" asked Silvio.

"C'mon, Uncle Coz, we're gonna be late."

Cosmo found his voice. "Sure, buddy. Hop in."

So I got into the passenger seat of his Camaro, and Cosmo moved to the driver's side. I heard Silvio say, "I'll come around another time, then."

"You do that, Sil."

Then Cosmo got in and started the car and we pulled away.

The interior of Cosmo's car was spotless. He had an air freshener in the shape of a pine tree hanging from the rearview mirror, which swung back and forth as we drove. It wasn't exactly a smooth ride, but since Mom and I had never owned a car ourselves and took buses everywhere we went, I decided to sit back, relax, and enjoy the experience.

We were quiet for a few moments, then Cosmo broke the silence. "Uncle Coz?"

I shrugged. "Coz. Cosmo. No matter how you slice it, it's a funny name."

"Excuse me?"

"Not funny *ha-ha*. Funny unusual. Like my name. Ambrose."

"No. Ambrose is funny *ha-ha*."

"No, it's not. It was my dad's name."

"Let me guess. He left because you were such a pain in the ass."

"No. He died."

It's amazing what those two words do to people when a kid my age is the one to say them. Sometimes I almost enjoy watching it happen. It was no different for Cosmo. He went really quiet, then he said, "I'm sorry."

"It's okay. It was before I was even born."

"What happened?"

"Brain aneurism. It just went *pop* one day."

"Is that why your mom's wound so tight?"

I hadn't thought of her that way before, but all I said was "I guess so."

"She's never met anyone else?"

"Not really. There was this professor she dated for a while in Regina, when I was younger. Phil. I liked Phil. But one day, she just stopped taking his calls."

"Huh."

"And there was a guy in Kelowna, but she only went out with him twice."

"You've moved a lot."

I shrugged. "She's a sessional lecturer. It's sort of like a professor without job security. We have to follow the work." I didn't tell him that, aside from the time she was fired, it was usually my mom's decision to pack up and leave; that after two or three years, she'd become disillusioned when she realized they were never going to offer her a full-time position. So she'd find yet another contract job in another university town.

I looked out my window at the houses that were getting bigger and nicer as we drove up the hill.

"You didn't really murder a kid, did you?"

"What do you think?"

"No."

"Well, you're right."

"Then why were you in jail, really?"

He hesitated, then he said, "I did some B and E's. Breaking and entering into people's houses."

"You stole their stuff?"

He nodded. "They let me off on probation the first time, but the second time the judge felt she needed to send me a message, so she sentenced me to six months."

"Wow. They let you off the first time and you did it again?"

Cosmo nodded.

"How dumb is that?"

He looked startled for a second, but then he laughed. "You have a point. Truth is, I also had a drug habit. I needed money to feed my addiction. It kind of won out over common sense."

"Are you still a druggie?" I asked, putting my hand on the door handle and calculating that I could always jump out at the next stop sign if it turned out he was driving high.

This made him laugh even harder. "A druggie?"

"Well, are you?"

"Technically, no. They got me into a rehab program while I was in jail. But I still go to NA meetings twice a week."

"NA?"

"Narcotics Anonymous."

"And that guy, Silvio, you knew him from before?"

Cosmo gripped the steering wheel tighter. "We were friends. And . . . business partners."

"Meaning, you broke into houses together."

"Yeah."

I looked at the tattoo on his arm. "That's an ugly tattoo."

He glanced at me. "And that's an ugly hat."

"My mom made it," I said, offended. "At least I can take it off."

"Fair enough," he said. "Now why don't you tell me, really, why you don't go a normal school?"

"I told you before. Three kids tried to kill me."

"The same three kids that were wailing on you the other day?"

"Yeah."

"They really tried to kill you?"

"I have a peanut allergy. They slipped a peanut into my sandwich, and I almost died."

He glanced over at me. "That sounds so weird, it must be true."

I peered out the window and saw a modern-looking blue church on the corner. "This is the place," I said.

Cosmo pulled up next to the curb. We both got out, and he immediately lit a cigarette. "Look, you did me a favor back there," he said, as he inhaled. "So find out how long it's going to be and I'll come back and pick you up when you're done."

"No. No way. You're coming in, too."

"No, I'm not."

"Yes, you are."

"No, I'm not —"

"Are you two looking for the Scrabble Club?" A woman was climbing out of a beat-up banana yellow Mazda across the street, carrying a stack of Scrabble boards. She was about Cosmo's age. She had shoulder-length red hair and a great body. She wore form-fitting jeans and the neatest sweater, with a giant sun on it. It didn't completely hide the fact that she had nice boobs.

In a word, she was spectacular. Cosmo must have thought so, too, because his mouth was hanging open and he was staring at her.

"The Scrabble Club," she repeated. "Are you looking for it?"

Cosmo stood mute beside me, so I said, "Yes."

"Well, you're in the right place. I'm Amanda. The club director. Come on in." She smiled and she had an overbite, which somehow made her even prettier.

I turned to Cosmo to convince him to come in with me, but I didn't have to.

He'd butted out his cigarette and was already following Amanda inside.

14

N R T T U A F S I O R

insofar, outfit, friars, fruits, futons

FRUSTRATION

he West Side Scrabble Club met in the church basement, in a large room that was normally used for Sunday school. I could tell because there were pictures hung all around the room of Baby Jesus being held by his mother, Mary; and Older Jesus playing with lambs, or talking to his disciples, or holding up fish and loaves of bread. On a blackboard at the front of the room, the words to the song "Jesus Loves the Little Children" were printed in neat letters, and the tables and chairs all had short legs. It looked a lot like the Sunday school I'd gone to in Regina once, when Mom had a brief religious phase. It lasted only for about six months, until she got bored, and we never went back.

"When did you two start playing Scrabble?" Amanda asked, as she set up a change box on a table by the entrance. Cosmo and I were the first players there.

I looked at Cosmo. All he said was "Only in the last year."

"I've been playing since I was eight," I said. "I beat my mom all the time."

"Well, here's how it works. You pay three dollars each to play three games –"

"Three games?" said Cosmo. "I don't know if we can stay that long."

"You have to stay for all three games, otherwise it messes up the rotation with the other players. We're normally here for about three hours."

"That's cool," I said quickly, calculating that, with Cosmo driving, I could still be home well before my mom. Then I smiled at Cosmo. "Can you lend me three bucks?"

He rolled his eyes, but I guess he didn't want to look like a cheapskate in front of Amanda because he paid for both of us.

"Our levels are beginner, intermediate, and expert," Amanda explained.

"You can put me in intermediate," I said proudly.

Amanda smiled and I noticed her cute overbite again. "I'm afraid you automatically go into beginner, kiddo. But if you win lots of games and enter a tournament or two, your ranking will go up pretty quickly. And we have quite a few beginners right now, so you'll get to play three different people tonight."

"Will I get to play you?" Cosmo asked Amanda, giving her a smile I had never seen before. The tough-guy stuff melted away and he suddenly looked boyish and almost charming.

"No," she laughed, "I'm in the intermediate level. C'mon, I'll show you where you can set up."

As she walked us to our table, Cosmo nudged me and hissed, "Take off your hat – you look like a dork." I stuck my tongue out at him, but I took it off and shoved it into my coat pocket.

Other people were trickling in now. They were a lot older than me, but aside from that, they were all different: fat, skinny, short, tall, white, brown, as young as Cosmo or as old as Nana Ruth. One woman was in a business suit and looked like she'd come straight from work. Lots of people were in jeans. A very large woman came dressed in different shades of pink from head to toe. A tall skinny guy with stooped shoulders wore sweatpants with sandals and no socks, even though it was damp and chilly outside. His sweatpants had mustard stains on them.

"I forgot to bring my board," I said to Amanda, as we arrived at our table.

"You don't need your board. I bring all the boards. They all have plastic tiles. Can you guess why?"

We both shrugged. She opened two Scrabble boxes and handed me a wooden tile from one set and a plastic tile from the other. "Feel them."

I did, then I passed them to Cosmo. "You can feel the letter on the wooden tile," he said. "It's indented a bit."

"That's right. Some players can actually figure out what letters they're grabbing, or recognize a blank tile." She sat us down and started setting up one of the club's boards. "Now, because you're just starting, you get what we call three weeks' grace. For three weeks, you can challenge your opponent's words without losing a turn, even if it ends up being a legitimate word. Ditto in reverse, if your opponent challenges one of your words and it isn't legitimate, you won't lose a turn. You're also allowed to use this 'cheat sheet' of all the accepted two-letter words."

She handed us a list. Some of them I recognized, but most of them I didn't. "Za?" I asked.

"Short for 'pizza,' believe it or not," she said.

"Get out," I replied.

"I kid you not," she laughed. "Now, if you go over your allotted twenty-five minutes, you won't be penalized. But after the first three weeks, you get ten points off your score for every minute you go over."

This was news to me. "We have a time limit?"

"Oh, yes. Otherwise the games could go on forever."

Games with my mom often did go on forever. "How do you know how much time you have?" I asked.

"These timers," she said, and she showed us a funny-looking box with two buttons on top and two digital displays that each read 25:00. "If you're the first player up, your opponent pushes your timer button the moment you look at your tiles. When you're done your turn, you call out your score, then you push your timer button, which stops your clock and starts your opponent's clock."

My stomach lurched. Mom and I never played with a clock, or even an hourglass. But by now it was seven, and Amanda was introducing us to the other beginners. I would be playing against Cosmo in my first game, then against an older guy named Mohammed, who had dark skin and a mustache and wore a Canucks jersey. My third opponent would be the enormous woman in pink. Her name was Joan.

I beat Cosmo easily. He kept glancing over at Amanda all the time, instead of paying attention to the game. In the end, our score was 242 to 173.

When it was time to play Mohammed, I was feeling a little more relaxed about the timer and a little more confident. "I beat my mom all the time," I told him.

"I beat my roommates all the time," he said. "In fact, they wouldn't play with me anymore, so I came here."

"You seem kind of old to have roommates," I said.

Cosmo, who was sitting next to me playing Joan, heard me and elbowed me, hard. "He has no filters," he said to Mohammed. "He just says what comes into his head."

But Mohammed just smiled and said, "It's okay." He went on to explain, "I used to have a wife, but she kicked me out, so now I have roommates."

We started to play. I was first to go and I laid down "TRIAL," which wasn't great because all the letters are only worth one point, but I laid the "T" on a double letter score and, being first up, I got to use the star in the middle for a double word score.

"Sixteen points," I said, and pushed the button to stop my clock. Mohammed almost immediately laid down "MIS" in front of "TRIAL" to create "MISTRIAL." The "M" was on the triple word score.

"Thirty points," he said, and he wrote it down because he was keeping score for both of us.

I put down "RUNNY" starting with the "R" in "TRIAL," and thanks to a double word score, I got another sixteen points.

Mohammed put down the word "QUILTS," adding an "S" to "MISTRIAL" and getting the points for both words (including a double letter score on the "Q"), for a score of thirty-seven points.

And that's how the game went, from one humiliation to the next. I challenged him a lot, on words like "YEGG," "TAXON," and "MIAOUS." Each time we'd walk over to a computer in the corner that was set up to the "Word Judge" program and punch in the word. They were all legitimate.

"That's so stupid," I grumbled. "It's not like anyone uses those words."

Mohammed shrugged. "If they're in the Word Judge, they count."

"It's still stupid," I muttered.

Mohammed won, 317 to 220. I had never been slaughtered like that.

"You wait," he said. "You'll get better. I was exactly like you when I first came here – a good kitchen player, but this . . ." He indicated the room. ". . . this was something completely different."

"I had really bad letters," I said.

My final game was with Joan. She used up all of her letters three times in one game. I found out there was a word for doing this – a "bingo." Each time, she got a bonus of fifty points. I must've challenged her on six words and, except for one, they were all legit.

"This is stupid. Whoever heard of 'CULTI'?"

"The Scrabble dictionary, that's who," Joan said. Then she laid down another bingo.

Beside us, Cosmo was done his game with Mohammed. He'd lost all three of his games, but it didn't seem to bother him. Amanda had to sit out her last game because they were short a player, and I saw Cosmo make a beeline for her and start chatting her up in the corner. He must've been saying funny things because she laughed a lot.

The final score of my game with Joan was a humiliating 385 to 223. I stood up so fast, I knocked my little chair over. I didn't bother picking it back up. I could see Joan and Mohammed whispering about me as Mohammed picked up my chair, but I didn't care. I just wanted to get out of there. I marched up to Cosmo, jamming my multicolored hat back onto my head.

"Let's go," I said.

"Will we see you next week?" Amanda asked. But I was already out the door.

In the car on the way home, Cosmo was humming. Actually humming.

"I don't see what you're so happy about," I finally said. "You lost all your games."

"So? I'll get better. Besides, it's just for fun."

"You mean, you're going back?" This surprised me and annoyed me all at once.

He shrugged. "Sure. And you are, too."

"No, I'm not."

"Yes, you are."

"No. I'm not."

"What? Baby doesn't want to go back because Baby wost his games?" He said this in a baby voice. "C'mon, Ambrose, you're made of tougher stuff than that."

"It was dumb. The people were dumb. Did you see Fatty all dressed up in pink? She looked like a giant cupcake."

"What does that have to do with anything? And no offense, but you're wearing a hat with a pom-pom. And I've avoided mentioning your purple cords."

"What's wrong with purple cords?" I loved my purple cords. I'd found them at Value Village and they were a perfect fit.

Cosmo opened his mouth to say something, then he closed it again. "Nothing. Nothing's wrong with your purple cords."

"I think they're classy," I said.

"Look, I saw how you played against me. You're good. Those other people just happen to be better. For now."

"You only want to go back because you've got a crush on Amanda."

He grinned. "Call it what you want. She was cute in the extreme."

"She's probably got a boyfriend."

"She doesn't. I asked."

"So you go back. You don't need me."

"Actually, I do. You're my beard."

"Your what?"

"My beard – my excuse." He hesitated for a second, then he confessed, "I told her I was your Big Brother."

"My big brother? We don't look remotely alike."

"Not that kind of big brother. A Big Brother. You know, the agency that matches up fatherless boys with guys who want to spend time with them. So they have a male role model."

I laughed really hard. I couldn't help myself. I laughed so hard, a snot-bubble came out my nose and I had to rub it on the sleeve of my coat.

"What's so funny?"

"The thought of you, as my role model."

"It's not that funny."

"Au contraire."

"C'mon, Ambrose. Go back with me next week."

"No."

"So is this the way you operate? Whenever the

going gets tough, Ambrose runs the other way?" He said this in a baby voice again.

"Shut up," I said.

"Good comeback," he retorted.

But then he did. Shut up, that is.

Neither of us said another word the rest of the way home.

15

R O I V S T I

sit, sort, visor, stir, sir, rots, riots, trios, iris, sort, visit

VISITOR

ut I guess a guy should never say "never" because, by the following Wednesday, I was even boreder, which I realize is not a word. But if some of the words used at the Scrabble Club were actual words, then I vote that "boreder" should be one too.

When my mom left for work, she said she might have a drink with Jane again. "I'll be home before midnight, and I'll have my cell."

"Great," I said. "Don't worry about me. I'll be

having another wild and crazy night at home with me, myself, and I, choosing what show to watch in our one-channel universe."

Her face crumpled and I regretted my words instantly.

"I'm doing the best I can, Ambrose."

"I know, Mom," I said quickly. "I know."

After she'd gone, I played solitaire until I heard Mr. and Mrs. E leave for their weekly dance night at the Greek Cultural Center, then I went outside and sat in the passenger seat of Cosmo's Camaro.

If he was surprised to see me when he stepped out at ten to seven, he didn't show it. He just got into the driver's seat, started the car, and said, "You pay for both of us this week."

I did even worse that night, losing all three games, including my game against Cosmo, which was truly humiliating.

"I had the worst letters ever," I told him, on the way home. "A monkey could have beat me with the letters I had."

Cosmo whistled under his breath. "Wow, little friend. I wouldn't have pegged you for a sore loser."

But even though I lost, something was beginning to click. I was starting to see the board differently, or at least, how some of my opponents, like Mohammed and Joan, looked at the board. And even though I was grumpy at the end, I definitely wasn't bored.

Now, during my evenings at home alone, I studied words. Amanda had photocopied some lists for me, and I studied all the two-letter words, plus "U"-less "Q" words, and "vowel dumps," words that use up a lot of vowels in a single turn.

On our fourth visit to the Scrabble Club, in early March, I won a game against Joan, thanks to playing the word "QWERTYS" on a triple word score, the "S" placed at the end of her word "SKUNK." I beat her 303 to 299, mainly because she had some tiles left over that were added to my score, but I didn't care. I still beat her, and I got my first-ever score in the 300's. The victory was so sweet, I leaped up and did a little dance on my chair, waving my arms around and chanting, "Uh-huh, uh-huh, uh-huh."

"Cool your jets, smarty-pants," Joan said to me.

"At least I fit into my pants," I said, under my breath.

When I looked at her, her face had gone kind of slack. For a moment, I wondered if she'd heard me.

But I decided she hadn't. She was just miffed that she'd lost against a twelve-year-old boy-wonder.

On our way home that night, Cosmo was humming again, even though he'd had another 3 to 0 losing streak.

"What are you doing Friday night?" he asked.

"Me? Nothing. Why?"

"I invited Amanda to go bowling with us."

"Us?"

"That's right."

"I hate bowling." I didn't add that I hated all sports.

"You've got something better to do?"

"I didn't say that."

The truth was, getting to go anywhere on a Friday night, even bowling, sounded better than another night at home watching CBC's "The National," their nightly newscast with Peter Mansbridge. Not that I had anything against Peter Mansbridge. In fact, I liked him a lot. His face and manner gave me comfort. Sometimes I even fantasized that he was my dad and that he would walk through the door around the same time as my mom. It was in a different, much bigger house that had rooms with names like "den" and "media room" and "solarium," and he would be tired after another night of delivering the news to Canadians, but not so tired that he wouldn't have time to chat with me about my day and make a date to play catch in the backyard. Then he and my mom would tuck me in and kiss me good night and go into their own bedroom, holding hands.

But then I would feel guilty about imagining anyone, other than my actual father, as my father.

"There's something you should know," Cosmo was saying. "She thinks it's one of our Big Brother activities."

I rolled my eyes. "Why did you ever tell her that?"

"I don't know. It was dumb. I wanted her to think –"

"That you're better than you are."

He laughed and gestured to himself. "Can you blame me?"

"No," I said, which, for some reason, made him laugh harder. "Does she know you smoke?"

"She's seen me smoking, yes."

"Does she know you're unemployed and living at home?"

"She knows I'm between jobs and temporarily staying with my parents."

"Does she know you're an ex-con and an ex-drug addict?"

"No," he said firmly. "And you're not going to tell her. I'll tell her when I'm ready."

We were quiet for a moment, then he said, with a hint of impatience, "Look, are you in or out?"

I was in, no matter what. But I saw a little window of opportunity and I ran with it. "I'm in on one condition," I said.

"What's that?"

"You teach me self-defense."

"Forget it."

"You said yourself I should learn."

"I meant a karate teacher, or tae kwon do, or something like that."

"We could never afford it. Plus, even if we could, Mom would never let me. She thinks it's violent."

"Then she wouldn't want me to teach you, either."

"Just a few moves? Please."

He sighed as we pulled into the driveway. "Well, I guess you of all people should learn to defend yourself."

"What do you mean – me of all people?"

He looked me right in the eye. "Face it, Ambrose. You rub a lot of people the wrong way."

"I do not." But I knew I did. "So it's a deal?"

"Deal," he said.

We shook on it. He had an extremely firm grip. I got out of the car, shaking the feeling back into my hand. I was just about to head around the side of the house to our apartment when Mrs. E stepped onto the porch, all dressed up in a matching floral skirt and blouse. I hadn't even noticed their car parked in the driveway. They weren't supposed to be home from the Greek Cultural Center yet. Thinking fast, I ducked out of sight, using the passenger side of the Camaro as my shield.

"Ma, you're home early," said Cosmo.

"Your father has a bad stomach," she said, as she hurried down the steps to join him. "That man, he came looking for you. Your old friend, Silvio."

Cosmo didn't say anything for a moment. "What did he want?"

"He said he needed to talk to you. I don't like him, Cosmo." Mrs. E sounded upset. "You told me you don't hang around with people like him anymore."

"I don't, Ma. I swear."

"He asked me to give you this." There was a brief silence, then the sound of someone scrunching up paper. I saw the balled-up wad hit the pavement on the driver's side.

"C'mon, Ma. Let's go inside."

I waited till I heard their front door close. Then I stood up and dashed around to the other side of the car and scooped up the ball of paper.

Once inside our apartment, I locked the door and got into my rocket-ship pajamas. Then I smoothed out the note.

There was only one word on it, and it wasn't a word I'd ever seen before, even at the Scrabble Club: "UOME."

It wasn't until later, when I was lying in bed staring at my glow-in-the-dark stars and waiting for my mom to come home, that I understood.

UOME. *You owe me.*

16

S T R A S B E

brass, stare, best, bears, bras, bass, rest, beast, bare

B R E A S T S

rs. E looked at me suspiciously when I showed up at their back door the next day at five, looking for Cosmo. Her hands were covered in flour and she was wearing an apron. I could see bread dough rising on the counter behind her.

"What are you two up to?" she asked, as we waited for Cosmo to appear.

"Cosmo's going to teach me self-defense," I said. "But maybe we don't need to mention it to my mom."

She studied me for a moment. "You're not doing anything naughty?"

"No, Mrs. E. You have my word."

"Then I see nothing." She winked at me and went back to her baking, just as Cosmo appeared. He was wearing a tank top and sweatpants.

"I hope you're not going to wear that on our date with Amanda," I said, as we headed into the backyard.

"*Our* date?" He cuffed me on the top of my head, but not too hard. "Tell you what. I won't wear these if you won't wear your hat. Or your purple cords."

"I told you, I like my purple cords. And my hat."

Cosmo took a deep breath, but all he said was "I know you do."

It was surprisingly mild for March, and the sun kept breaking through the clouds. Purple and yellow crocuses were sprouting up all over their garden. Cosmo had strung up an old punching bag to the branch of a maple tree. He held on to it while I punched. I'd always wanted to hit a punching bag, but I was surprised at how much it hurt. It hurt a lot.

"It'll get easier as you build your strength," Cosmo said.

I looked at his muscular arms, then at my own

toothpick arms, and I felt a sudden wave of hopeless-
ness. "Maybe we shouldn't bother," I said.

"Don't be ridiculous. It's like improving your
Scrabble game. It takes time. Now get down and give
me twenty-five push-ups."

Twenty-five push-ups just about killed me, but we
were far from over.

"Now I'm going to teach you a few blocks," he said.

"I don't want to learn blocks. I want to learn how
to fight back," I said, although, at that moment, all
I really wanted to do was retreat to my room and have
a nap.

"One step at a time, Ambrose. Now, try to punch
me in the face."

"I can't do that –"

"Sure you can."

So I tried to punch him.

Cosmo swiftly brought up his right arm, bent at the
elbow, and easily blocked my fist. "You can do better
than that. Put some force into it."

So I tried again, harder this time, and he easily
blocked my fist again. "No offense, Ambrose, but you
swing like a girl," he said.

"Offense taken," I retorted.

He showed me high blocks and low blocks.
"Blocking is your number one line of defense against

jerks like those bullies at your old school," he told me. "Now, try to block my punch."

Cosmo swung at me, not too hard, and I quickly brought my arm up.

"I did it!" I shouted. "I blocked your punch!" But in my excitement, I didn't see the next one coming. He hit me in the stomach. I doubled over, winded but not hurt.

"*Geez*, Ambrose, I'm sorry," he said, as I got my breath back. "Are you okay?"

I nodded – then I punched Cosmo in the stomach, taking him by surprise. He looked more startled than hurt, then he burst out laughing. "You're a fast learner," he said, and I felt a bubble of pride well up inside me.

Cosmo decided we'd done enough upper-body stuff after that. I was ready to call it quits, but he took a soccer ball out of the shed instead.

"I don't play soccer. I hate soccer."

"You've never played it."

"Because I hate it."

"You hate it because you're afraid you might embarrass yourself."

"I'm not afraid I might embarrass myself. I know I'm going to embarrass myself. It's happened many times."

"Well, you can't be embarrassed in front of me."

So we kicked the ball around for a while and I was terrible, but he was right. I didn't feel embarrassed. Near the end I actually managed one beautiful kick, and Cosmo high-fived me. A little jolt went through my stomach because, outside of gym, I'd never kicked a ball of any type around with anyone, except maybe once or twice with Phil, before my mom stopped taking his calls.

When we'd put the soccer ball away, Cosmo lit up a cigarette.

"You keep your car spotless, but you fill your body with poison," I said, watching him.

"This is my only addiction right now," he replied. "In my books, I'm doing pretty good."

"Why did you start using drugs?"

He shrugged. "I was messed up. I didn't know what to do with my life."

"I don't know what to do with my life, and I don't do drugs."

He smiled. "It's complicated. I was depressed. And angry. And confused. . . . A friend offered me something at a party one night and it made me feel a lot better. For a while, the drugs kept making me feel better. Then they made me feel worse, but by then I was addicted." He ground out his cigarette. "What can I say, Ambrose? There's a lot of paths to choose from in life. I took a wrong turn."

"What do you owe Silvio?"

"What?"

"UOME. I read the note."

"What'd you do that for?"

"You left it beside the car. It was tempting."

"You're such a wiener."

"Are you going to tell me, or not?"

Cosmo sighed. "I owe him some money."

"How much?"

"Two grand."

I whistled, or tried to. I've never really mastered whistling. "That's a lot."

"He loaned it to me just before I did that last B and E. We were supposed to do the job together, but he didn't show up, so I did it alone. I figured I'd sell a bunch of the stuff I stole and get him his money back. But that's not what happened."

"What did happen?"

"I didn't know the owners had a dog."

"A Doberman pinscher? A German shepherd?"

"A Labradoodle."

"A Labradoodle?"

"Labrador crossed with poodle. Tiny little thing."

"You're kidding me."

"I wish."

"So what happened?"

"I was high, which was my first mistake. I was carrying this big flat-screen TV to the back door and, next thing you know, this little pup came tearing out of nowhere. I tripped over him and knocked myself out on a corner of the TV. I guess the owners came home because, when I came to, the cops were already there."

"Wow. That's kind of . . ."

"Embarrassing? Yeah. What can I say: Crime doesn't pay."

"Supper's ready!" Mrs. E called from the back door. "And Ambrose, I insist you stay. Peanut-free," she added with a laugh, and I suspected she was having a little fun at my mother's expense.

Cosmo and I walked toward the house.

"Was the Labradoodle okay?" I asked.

"The Labradoodle was fine. Now shut up about it and let's eat."

Mom noticed I was acting awfully perky as she headed off to work on Friday. "You're in a good mood," she said, as I spun her around to a song on our boom box called "Darlin'." It was a peppy, countryish number by a Canadian band – Luther Wright and the Wrongs – and it was on one of my mom's favorite CD's. When our budget would allow it, she'd pick up interesting music from a used CD shop on West 4th Avenue.

"Fridays," I said, as the song ended. "'Royal Canadian Air Farce' on CBC. Who wouldn't be in a good mood?"

"By the way," she said, as she put a bunch of term papers into her bag, "I found out why Cosmo was in prison."

My stomach did a flip. "Oh, yeah?"

"Mrs. Economopoulos told me. I guess she felt I should know, which was good of her."

"So?"

"He got caught breaking into someone's house. To support a drug habit." She shook her head, disgusted.

"But he's not on drugs anymore," I said.

She stopped what she was doing and looked at me. "How on earth would you know?"

"Well, he doesn't seem like he is."

She put on her brown suede jacket that she'd got for only twenty bucks at Goodwill and that looked amazing on her. "His mother says he isn't using anymore, either." By the way she said it, I could tell she didn't believe it.

"Why are you so skeptical?" I said. "Maybe he really *is* clean. Maybe he really *is* trying to make a new start for himself. Maybe he's really a good guy who took a wrong turn."

She looked puzzled. "Why do you care so much?"

"I don't. I'm just saying, you shouldn't always expect the worst in people."

She put her hands on my shoulders. "Ambrose. I

don't mean to expect the worst. But in my experience, the worst is what often happens." That hung in the air. *Had she always felt this way,* I wondered, *or was it only after "the worst" had happened to my dad?*

"Believe me," she continued, "I sincerely hope that he's managing to stay clean. Because if he falls off the wagon, he might try to steal from us, too."

"We have nothing to steal."

"Drug addicts don't care about that. Mrs. Economopoulos told me he used to steal money from her wallet all the time."

I thought about the jar of quarters in my room.

Mom put on the floppy hat with the flower on it, then she held out her arms and I gave her a hug and a kiss. "I'm going to have a drink with Jane after our classes," she said. "I'll be home by midnight."

Once she left, I went into my bedroom and hid my quarter collection under my bed. Just to be safe.

At six o'clock, Cosmo picked me up in his Camaro at the end of our block. Having dinner and getting self-defense lessons from him in the backyard were secrets the Economopouloses didn't seem to mind keeping, but I figured going out with Cosmo in his sports car on a Friday night would be pushing the envelope.

"You look good," I said. He was wearing new-looking jeans and a short-sleeve button-up shirt that partially hid his tattoo.

"Thanks. You look . . . unique. Quite bright."

I'd opted to wear my good pants – the brown ones that were a bit tight in the crotch but otherwise perfect – my Ikes, and a neon green T-shirt that I felt brought out the flecks of green in my brown eyes.

"You washed the car too," I said.

"Inside and out."

"Funny how you take better care of your car than you do of your own self."

He just gave me the stink-eye.

But as we drove through the neighborhood streets to pick up Amanda, who lived in a low-rise apartment building near 4th and Burrard, I could hardly breathe. "What's that smell?" I asked, unrolling my window.

"My aftershave," said Cosmo.

"What'd you do, pour it over your head?"

"Is it too much?"

"Yes!"

So Cosmo turned the car around and I ducked down in the passenger seat as he ran back into the house to shower and change. I'd never seen him like this before.

Once he was back in the car, I asked him: "Have you ever fallen off the wagon?"

"What?"

"With the drugs, since you got out of jail."

"No. I was tempted at the beginning, but no."

"Promise?"

"Where is this coming from?"

"Would you steal from us?"

"What the hell are you talking about?"

"You stole from your mom."

"*Aw*, for – yes. I did. When I was using. I'm not now. That part of my life is over, understood?"

I wanted to ask him how he could be sure, but we'd arrived outside Amanda's apartment building. She was waiting out front, and even to my untrained eye, I could see she looked drop-dead gorgeous in a peasant top with a plunging neckline, a short brown leather jacket, and a pair of tight jeans tucked into red cowboy boots. She smiled at us and headed toward the car.

"Get your ass into the backseat," Cosmo said, as he climbed out to open the door for Amanda, a big goofy grin on his face.

— 17 —

N N B I D O G

bingo, boing, bind, doing, big, bog, ding, dong, gob

BONDING

osmo wanted to take us to a Chinese place next to the bowling alley for some supper first, but I told him I probably shouldn't eat there with my allergy because some of the dishes would have peanuts in them.

"So we'll order the dishes without peanuts," said Cosmo.

"No, he's right," said Amanda. "With an allergy like that, you can't be too careful. Even if they used the same wok, or if a stray peanut got in . . . that's all it takes."

I gave Cosmo a smug look and Amanda my biggest smile. She ruffled my hair, which felt good. "I have a cousin with a peanut allergy," she explained.

So Cosmo took us for pizza instead. It was quite a thrill for me, being in the brightly lit, noisy restaurant. Mom and I almost never ate out, because it was a) expensive and b) too stressful because of my allergy.

Amanda ordered a beer and Cosmo and I ordered large Cokes. Cosmo used the excuse that he was driving, but I wondered if being an ex-druggie meant he wasn't allowed to drink, either.

Amanda asked Cosmo how long he'd been my Big Brother.

Cosmo coughed. "Not too long," he said.

"Well, you seem like an awfully good match."

"Oh, yes," I said, milking it. "Cosmo's very generous. He loves taking me out to things I've never tried before, since I don't have a dad and all. Next Friday night, he's promised to take me to Cliffhanger."

Cosmo almost choked on his bread stick.

"The climbing gym?" said Amanda. "I've always wanted to try that."

"I'm sure Cosmo wouldn't mind if you came along, would you, Cosmo?"

Cosmo forced a smile. "We'd love it if you'd join us." Then he kicked me hard under the table.

"I'd like that. But how can you afford it, if you're between jobs?"

"It isn't easy," Cosmo answered. "But I do it for the boy." He slapped me on the back, a little harder than he needed to.

"What about you, Amanda?" Cosmo asked.

"What about me?"

"What do you do when you're not playing Scrabble?"

"Well . . . I knit."

"You knit?"

Amanda smiled. "I work at Wild and Woolly on Main Street."

I knew Main Street. Mom and I had gone there once on a Saturday outing. It was a really neat part of town, full of funky shops selling antiques and clothes, and a bakery that sold the best chocolate-chip cookies ever.

"It's a knitting shop," she explained. "And twice a week, I host Stitch and Bitch sessions at my apartment for a little extra cash."

"Stitch and Bitch?" I asked.

"Yeah, I normally have about ten people per session, usually all women. We barely fit into my apartment and we all work on a special knitting project."

"Did you knit that sweater you were wearing when we first met you?" I asked. "The one with the big sun?"

"I sure did," she said. "I knit everything." She showed us her belt and her purse, both made from colorful wools. "I sell my stuff in a few shops. It doesn't make me rich, but you know what they say, 'Follow your heart. . . .'" She laughed like she was embarrassed.

"I'd like to follow my heart," Cosmo said. "If only I could figure out where it wants to go."

She gave him a sweet smile, then she turned to me. "Speaking of knitting, how come you aren't wearing your cool hat tonight?"

"You like my hat?"

"Yeah, I do. Someone made it for you, right?"

I shot Cosmo a triumphant look, then nodded. "My mom."

"Tell her if she ever wants to come to one of my Stitch and Bitch groups, she's welcome."

"Sure," I lied. "I'll tell her."

She turned back to Cosmo and said, almost shyly, "I also like your tattoo." Then Amanda pulled back the neck of her blouse, revealing a small, bright blue dragonfly tattoo on her shoulder blade. "I'm thinking of getting another one, on my ankle."

It was Cosmo's turn to shoot me a triumphant look. "The dragonfly looks beautiful on you," he said. They smiled at each other and this time it was long and lingering and mushy, so I decided to change the subject.

"How did you get into Scrabble?" I asked.

"Oh, I've always loved Scrabble. I played all through high school. I was a total nerd," she giggled.

"I find that hard to believe," said Cosmo.

"No, I really was. You should see my yearbook photo."

"I'd like that."

They looked at each other in that way again and Amanda blushed. "Anyway, I joined the West Side Scrabble Club a few years back, and when the club director moved to Kamloops, they needed someone new to step in, so . . . here I am."

"You're an excellent club director," I said, laying it on a little thick. "Top-notch."

"Well, thank you very much, Ambrose," she said, taking a sip of her beer. "You know, as club director, one of the more difficult jobs I have is trying to keep the peace among all the different players with their different personalities."

"I can imagine," I said. "Like Larry, the expert guy, and the way he's always clearing phlegm from his throat. I can hear him from across the room. And Joan, the fat lady in pink."

"Funny you should mention Joan," said Amanda. "She told me you said something rather cruel to her the other night."

So she had heard me. "I don't know what you're

talking about," I said, but I could feel my whole face go hot, even my ears.

"Did you say something about her not being able to fit into her pants?"

Cosmo snorted and Coke came out of his nose.

I pondered how to answer this. In the end I didn't answer, which was pretty much like answering, if you know what I mean.

"You can't do that, Ambrose," Amanda said, kind of gentle but kind of firm. "You can't make disparaging remarks. Imagine how you'd feel if someone did that to you."

"You, of all people, should know that," Cosmo chimed in. "Those guys at your old school, weren't they always picking on you and calling you names?"

I gave him the stink-eye. Cosmo was shameless, suddenly acting like he *was* my Big Brother, just to impress Amanda.

Our pizza arrived, but I wasn't feeling so hungry anymore. "I'm sorry," I mumbled. "It won't happen again."

"Good," said Amanda, "because if it did, I'd be forced to ask you to leave the club, and that would be a shame because I really like having you there." She smiled at me and I could tell she was trying to make me feel better. "But since we're on the topic, there are a few other things you need to know. Number One – nobody likes to hear another player gripe about lousy letters."

"I couldn't agree more," said Cosmo.

Amanda ignored him, which gave me a bit of satisfaction. "Everyone gets lousy letters once in a while, and it all evens out in the end. It's just a game, deal with it. Number Two – the only thing worse than a sore loser is a sore winner."

"*Ha!* Didn't I tell you?" said Cosmo smugly, which made me want to hit him.

"So no more victory dances on the chairs, okay?"

"Okay," I said. I was worried I was going to cry, when Amanda reached over and put her arm around me and pulled my head right into her boobs.

"I've made you sad, and that was not my intention, kiddo. I'm only telling you like it is because I think you can handle it and because I like you."

She let me go. My head was spinning. I'm sure I had a silly look on my face.

"And because I think you could be a really good player. You just have to remember that playing competitive Scrabble is different from playing kitchen Scrabble. I read this great book about Scrabble last year, called *Word Freak* by Stefan Fatsis, and he says Scrabble isn't about words, it's about mastering the rules of the game." She patted my hand.

"Will you help me?" I asked, trying to look at her face and not at where my head had just been.

"Sure I will. In fact, I brought you a present." She pulled a dog-eared book out of her bag and handed it to me. "It's the *Official Scrabble Tournament and Club Word List*," she said. "Different from the *Official Scrabble Dictionary* for home players. This one has all the swear words." She winked. "I had an extra one kicking around."

"Thanks," I said, and I meant it. I had my appetite back, and I grabbed a piece of pizza. It was delicious – better by far than Mom's homemade whole-wheat crust pizza.

"What about me?" asked Cosmo. "Do you think I can be a good player?"

Amanda smiled. "I think you can be as good as you want to be, but that you don't care enough to become very good. I think your motives are suspect."

Cosmo helped himself to a second piece of pizza. "That sounds about right," he said, and for some reason this got him a big huge *aren't you just the cutest thing on earth* grin from Amanda.

After pizza, we went bowling. I'd bowled only once before, at one of the few birthday parties I'd ever been invited to. It was in Regina and, now that I think about it, the whole class had been invited. We were divided into teams, and I kept sending my balls into the gutter and making my teammates groan. Then right at the end of the party, I barfed all over the floor because I'd wolfed down too many hot dogs, since Mom would never buy hot dogs because she thought they were disgusting.

Tonight, though, I wasn't that bad. Not as good as Amanda, who was really good, bowling strike after strike. I got a couple of gutters, but most of the time I'd knock down a pin or two. Once I got a strike and just about screamed like a girl, I was so pleased. Cosmo sucked, although I think a bit of it was for show. Every time he sent another ball into the gutter, Amanda would double over with laughter, and I could tell he liked making her laugh.

At ten o'clock, I excused myself and called my mom from the bathroom on my cell phone to make sure she was still going out with Jane.

"I'm planning on it, but only if it's okay with you," she said.

"No problem, Mom. Go for it. Just don't drink and drive, *ha-ha.*"

At eleven o'clock, we drove Amanda home. When we arrived outside her apartment, Cosmo asked me to wait in the car while he walked her to the door.

I got back into the front seat and watched them. They chatted for a few minutes, and I thought they were going to leave it at that, when suddenly Cosmo leaned in and kissed her. I waited for her to push him away, but she didn't. In fact, she put her arms around him and kissed right back. They must've kissed for over a minute. I bent forward to get a better view and accidentally hit the horn. They jumped away from each other, and, a moment later, Cosmo returned to the car.

"What'd you do that for?"

"It was an accident."

Cosmo waited until Amanda was not only safely inside the building, but safely inside her apartment. We saw the lights go on in a unit on the second floor, then she stepped out onto her balcony and waved at us.

Cosmo waved back. Then he put the car into gear and we drove off. He was humming again.

"She's great," I said.

"She sure is."

"Great smile."

"Yup."

"Cute overbite."

"Uh-huh."

"Fabulous boobs."

He reached over and slugged me.

"Ow!"

He just kept humming.

"I think she's looking forward to doing indoor rock climbing with us next Friday," I said.

"Yeah, thanks a lot for that. Do you have any idea how much a place like that costs?"

I shrugged. "Then I guess you'd better get serious about finding a job."

18

STHYNOE

nest, notes, tones, hones, honey, stony, shone, then, hey

HONESTY

I won two out of my three games, both with scores over 300, at the Scrabble Club the following Wednesday. And I was on my best behavior, too. No complaints about lousy letters (even though it killed me not to say something when my seven tiles were OUIIOUK); no victory dances when I won. But it was impossible to keep from grinning when I managed to beat Joan again.

"You could wipe that smile off your face," Joan said.

"I'm sorry," I replied. "I'm only smiling because it means a lot to me to beat someone who's as good as you. And have I ever told you, pink is really your color?"

Okay, I laid it on a bit thick, but I think she liked it because she smiled.

In the evenings, I studied the *Official Scrabble Tournament and Club Word List,* which was an interesting book because it didn't give definitions. It just listed column after column of words, and I only recognized about half of them on each page. And it really was full of all the swears. I discovered that there are ten different ways you can legitimately use the "f" word.

On Friday, Mom told me she and Jane were going out for a drink again after classes. Needless to say, I didn't give her any grief this time. When she left, Cosmo gave me another self-defense lesson. I still wasn't great, but I was better than last time and, as Cosmo kept reminding me, that was what counted.

When we were done, I showered and changed for our evening out. As we drove to pick up Amanda, I asked him how he was going to pay for everything. "I'd rather wait and tell you both," he replied.

Cliffhanger was a blast. My mom had never let me do anything this physical because she was worried I'd get hurt, so my arms were killing me after only three climbs. But I kept on going. It was exhilarating and terrifying all at once, being so high off the ground, even though I knew I was perfectly safe with an instructor belaying me below. Amanda and Cosmo were having a great time too, and I saw them steal a couple of kisses between climbs.

Near the end of our session, Cosmo managed to get to the top of a climb that was rated "eight" in difficulty. When he was done, he grinned from ear to ear. "Now *that* was a good high," he said, to no one in particular.

At the restaurant afterward, a burger joint with an arcade near the front, Cosmo said he had an announcement. "I got a job," he told us.

"Hey, that's great!" Amanda said.

"Doing what?" I asked.

"Working construction. A friend of my brother-in-law's is the foreman on this big project downtown. I'll be picking up shifts here and there to start, but I'm hoping, once I prove myself, it will grow into full-time work."

"This calls for a toast," said Amanda. We all raised our glasses and clinked them together.

"You ever wonder why they call buildings buildings?" I asked. "Shouldn't they be called builts?"

This made them laugh and then our burgers came and they were delicious. After we ate, Cosmo gave me a bunch of loonies to play in the games room attached to the restaurant. Mom never let me play those games, and even though I knew he only did it because he wanted to be alone with Amanda, I didn't care.

I got kind of addicted to the racing car game. I played it over and over again to see if I could stay on the track longer than a minute without crashing. I'd just managed to get to almost two minutes (my own personal record) when my cell phone rang. I looked at the call display.

It was Mom, calling from her cell phone.

Thinking fast, I left my game halfway through and ducked into the men's washroom. "Hi, Mom," I said.

"Where are you? Why didn't you pick up at home?"

"I am home," I lied. "I couldn't make it to the phone the first time. I was having a dump."

"*Ugh,* too much information," she said. "Listen, Jane canceled. She's not feeling well."

I looked at my watch. It was 10:15. My stomach did a flip. "Where are you?"

"Just walking to the bus stop. I should be home in twenty minutes."

My stomach did a double flip.

"I thought we could be rebels and stay up late, play a game of Scrabble."

"Sounds great," I said, feeling queasy. "See you soon." I hung up.

Then I tore back to our table, where Cosmo and Amanda were holding hands. "Cosmo, we've gotta get out of here," I blurted. "My mom's on her way home."

"I don't understand," Amanda said, as Cosmo grabbed the waiter and handed him a fifty-dollar bill. "His mother doesn't know he's out with you?"

"Not exactly," said Cosmo, and I could see little beads of sweat popping out on his forehead.

"You took a twelve-year-old boy out for the evening without his mom's knowledge?"

"It's not – you're making it sound like something it isn't," Cosmo said, as we all hurried to the door.

"Well, what is it then? His mom trusts you. You're his Big Brother."

"Not technically," I said, as we rushed through the parking lot to Cosmo's car.

"Thanks, Ambrose," Cosmo replied, in a way that I was pretty sure was sarcastic.

"You're not his Big Brother?" said Amanda, her voice suddenly kind of strangled. "You lied to me?"

"No. Yes. A little white lie. I just – I wanted to go out with you," he confessed, as we all piled into the car.

"So you lied," she said. "And used a twelve-year-old boy –"

"He didn't use me." I wanted to help Cosmo. "I used him. I got him to drive me to Scrabble Club. He's my upstairs neighbor."

Amanda raised an eyebrow as we pulled out of the parking lot.

"And he acts like my Big Brother – he does all the stuff a Big Brother should. In fact, it's too bad Big Brothers does background checks because they'd be lucky to have a guy like Cosmo."

Cosmo groaned.

"Background checks?" Amanda was almost whispering now. "What else haven't you told me?"

"I was going to tell you everything," Cosmo said.

"When?"

"Soon. Soonish."

"How about now." Suddenly her voice was not the sweet Amanda voice we'd come to know and love. It was like steel.

Cosmo took a deep breath. "Fine. I'm living with my parents because I just got out of jail. I was in for six months for a string of B and E's, which I did to support a drug habit. And no, I'm not really Ambrose's Big Brother, but when I saw you that first night, I would have said anything for a chance to spend a little more time with you."

Amanda didn't say a word. She was so angry, she was practically vibrating. I could feel the anger coming off her in waves, even from my spot in the backseat. But there was nothing I could do about it because, as we turned onto our block, I saw my mom coming from the other direction, walking home from the bus stop.

I groaned. "I am so doomed."

"Duck," Cosmo said.

I did. And he drove right past my mom, around the corner, and into the back alley behind the house. "Now, run," he said, and I did. I leapt out of the car and dashed through the back gate and fumbled with my keys. I made it through the door and flipped on the light. I threw myself onto the couch and grabbed the remote and put on the CBC, just as Mom entered.

"Hi," I said. "Still want to play Scrabble?"

"Sure," she replied, a bit wearily.

She took off her shoes, then went to the fridge to get a bottle of wine. "I think I just saw Cosmo drive by with a young woman in the car." She shook her head. "I pity that poor girl. I bet, dollars to doughnuts, she has no idea what she's getting into."

Saturday morning, I woke up in a foul mood. I was so crabby that, after we'd done our laundry, Mom suggested she go for our beach walk by herself. I responded that I thought that was a really good goddamn idea, which made her tell me to watch my mouth, which made me tell her that that was like the pot calling the kettle black, which made her say, "Oh, for Chrissakes!" which made me say, "See?" all triumphant-like, which made her say, "I hope to hell you're in a better mood when I get back," which made me say, "You just swore again," which made her storm out of the house.

The moment she was gone, I called upstairs. Disguising my voice, I asked for Cosmo.

"Ambrose, is that you?" Mrs. E said.

"Ambrose? Who's Ambrose?" I said, still disguising my voice.

"We have call display," she replied.

"Oh, *Ambrose*," I said, pretending I'd just understood her. "Sorry, I have a cold. Can I talk to Cosmo?"

She put Cosmo on the line and he agreed to meet me in the backyard in five minutes. He was in sweatpants and a sweatshirt. It looked like he hadn't slept much. He lit a cigarette, even though he probably hadn't even had breakfast yet. I decided this wasn't the time to bug him about it.

"What happened?" I asked.

"I drove her home. I told her it would never happen again, I was sorry, I was in Narcotics Anonymous, *blah-blah-blah*. She just jumped out of the car."

"I'm sorry, Cosmo," I said, and I could feel my eyes prickling with tears. "It's all my fault."

"What are you talking about? It's my fault, okay?" He squeezed my shoulder. "I'm the one who lied to her."

"Have you sent her flowers?"

"No."

"You should send her flowers. I read this magazine in the doctor's office once that said women like that."

"I don't know. She was pretty pissed."

"You can't just give up," I said.

He inhaled deeply on his cigarette. "Fine. I'll send flowers. And now I've got to get some coffee." He turned to go into the house.

"What about Scrabble Club?"

He turned back. "I guess it's on hold for now. Sorry, Ambrose."

I could feel my eyes welling up with tears again. "Can we still do self-defense? I mean, I know you were only hanging out with me because of Amanda, so if you don't —"

"Is that what you think?"

I nodded.

"Then you're even dumber than you look."

He cuffed my head. And even though it hurt a bit, it also felt really good.

19

R S C N A O I T C

arctic, accost, carotin, action, cacti, cat

NARCOTICS

osmo sent flowers to Amanda that morning, but he didn't hear from her. On Monday he told me that he'd tried to call her a couple of times, but she wasn't home or just wasn't answering.

When he still hadn't heard from her by Wednesday, he refused to go to Scrabble Club. I missed it even more than I thought I would. I went upstairs to see if Cosmo wanted to play Scrabble, just the two of us, but Mrs. E told me he was out.

"At an NA meeting," she said.

I waited to hear his car pull up so I could go and talk to him, but he still hadn't shown up by the time Mom came home.

On Friday, after my mom left for work, I knocked on the back door for my self-defense lesson. Cosmo answered, wearing his tank top and sweatpants. He looked rough and kind of jittery, and he was halfway through a cigarette.

"Do your parents let you smoke in the house?" I asked, because I knew they didn't.

"They're not home," he replied, crabby-like.

"They'll be able to smell it —"

"Ambrose. Lay off, okay?"

I looked at his outfit. "Did you work today?"

"No. They haven't been needing me as much as I'd hoped."

"That's too bad." There was an awkward silence for a moment, then I said, "I've been working on my blocks. I think I'm getting better."

"Yeah, about that. I can't work out with you today." He wouldn't look me in the eye. "I have to go out."

"Where to?"

"Not your business."

"If you could just give me a hint. . . ."

"Ambrose —"

"Or I could go with you."

"Jesus, Ambrose, back off. I'll see you later, okay?"
He closed the door.

I had a bad feeling. A very bad feeling. So instead
of going back to our apartment, I ran around to the
front of the house and climbed into Cosmo's car.
I crawled into the backseat and crouched down on
the floor.

A few minutes later, Cosmo got in the car and we
pulled away.

We'd been driving for close to half an hour. My legs
were cramped and sore, and the waistband of my pants
was biting into my flesh, cutting off my circulation. I
started to worry that if I stayed like this long enough,
they'd have to amputate me from the waist down. This
thought started to freak me out and I decided that I had
to shift my position, so I waited until a car horn honked
loudly nearby and I moved.

From my new position, I could just barely see out
the back window. I could tell we were in a rough part of
town. There were boarded-up buildings and some
tragic, scary-looking people wandering around, people
who looked more like zombies than human beings. A
couple of them wandered into traffic like they didn't
care if they lived or died. To be honest, I felt scared. I
wished I'd just stayed home.

I don't know if it was fear, or something I ate, but suddenly I had to fart something fierce. I let it out slowly, silently. But even if Cosmo couldn't hear it, he couldn't help but smell it. All the windows were closed.

"*Aw*, gross," I heard him mutter up front. I hoped he might open his window, but he must've thought the smell was coming from outside because the window stayed shut.

Just when I started to worry I might get carsick, Cosmo pulled over to the curb. I ducked down and felt a rush of cool air as he opened his window.

"Hey. Got anything today?" I heard him say.

Next thing I knew, two messed-up looking guys – one with long greasy hair and the other one with no hair at all because he'd shaved his head bald and had a huge tattoo on it of a hand gripping his forehead – were at the window. I tried to make myself smaller.

"Whatcha looking for?" asked tattoo-guy.

"Whatever you got," said Cosmo.

"Long as you got the cash, we can set you up," said tattoo-guy, and he reached into his pocket.

Suddenly greasy-hair-guy looked in the backseat and locked eyes with me. "You want some for the kid, too?"

Oh, man.

Cosmo turned slowly in his seat. I sat up and gave him a feeble wave. "Oh, hi," I said.

Anger flashed through Cosmo's eyes. For a moment, I felt scared of him and scared of what he might do. But just as quickly, the anger disappeared and he looked a little deflated.

"Never mind," he said to the two guys.

He pulled away from the curb. I could hear the two guys yelling as we drove off.

Cosmo was quiet for a few minutes, then he said, "You might as well ride up front." So I climbed over the seat and sat beside him and buckled up my seat belt and locked my door because I still felt scared.

"Is there an NA meeting today?" I asked him.

"There's always an NA meeting."

"I think we should go."

"Ambrose. It's called Narcotics *Anonymous*."

"Okay, then. You go. I'll wait in the car."

He glanced at me and shook his head. "You are one of a kind."

"Is that a compliment?"

"It's an observation."

Cosmo knew of an NA meeting taking place in Kerrisdale, another neighborhood on the west side of Vancouver, so we drove up there together. It was a beautiful early April day, so I went to the nearby park and sat on a bench to wait for him, eating the jumbo bag of chips Cosmo had bought for me and thinking.

Contrary to what my fourth-grade teacher had once said to me, I wasn't a total idiot. I knew I couldn't watch Cosmo 24/7. I knew that if he really wanted to do drugs again, it would be impossible for me to stop him.

So I had to think of things that would take his mind off drugs. Things that would make him feel better about life, and about himself.

When he came out, I told him, "I have a plan."

"A plan for what?"

"A plan for you to win Amanda back."

"This is crazy," Cosmo said, as we stood outside Amanda's apartment the next night.

"No," I corrected him. "It's romantic."

We were wearing matching tuxedo T-shirts that I'd found at Goodwill that afternoon. I'd bought them with some of my quarter collection. Cosmo clutched a bouquet of flowers.

There were lights on in Amanda's apartment, so we were pretty sure she was home. Lucky for us, her balcony doors were open a crack. A pink bicycle with knitted handlebar covers sat on the balcony, along with a bunch of potted plants.

I put my mom's boom box on the pavement and handed Cosmo a lyric sheet.

"Ready?"

"No."

I pressed PLAY and suddenly Luther Wright's voice filled the air. I had it cued up to "Darlin'," and the machine was cranked up to full volume. Cosmo and I started to sing along.

"Darlin' when you love me I feel home sweet home . . ."

Except Cosmo was mumbling instead of singing, so I hit the STOP button. "C'mon, you've gotta belt it out. Sing it like you mean it," I said.

A few people were eyeing us curiously from the sidewalk as they passed, enjoying the pleasant spring evening. Cosmo's face had turned beet red. "I can't do this."

"Why not?"

"Because I'm going to look like a total moron."

"Maybe. But, at this point, she already thinks you're a total moron, so what have you got to lose?"

He sighed. "Point taken. Let's get it over with."

I hit PLAY again and this time Cosmo belted out the lyrics with me. His voice was, well, crappy, which had me a little worried. An old man stopped to gawk, and in Amanda's apartment building, a few people stepped out onto their balconies.

"There's nothing we can't talk about, like the last time we had it out, and that's the truth. And I lost a tooth," we sang. "I lost a tooth" was my favorite line, and I thought it showed we had a sense of humor, too.

Just when I was starting to worry that everyone in the building was hearing our song except Amanda, a woman poked her head out of Amanda's balcony doors. Only it wasn't Amanda. Then a few more women stepped out onto the balcony. They were all holding knitting needles and half-finished sweaters and scarves. It dawned on me that Amanda must be having one of her Stitch and Bitch sessions. Cosmo's face had gone even redder, which I didn't think was possible, but he kept on singing.

"You say you like the way it makes me smile. And even if I can't chew my food, it's nothing compared to what I'd do to be with you."

Some of the women started to laugh.

"Amanda, you'd better get out here," one of them called.

Finally Amanda herself stepped out. She looked gorgeous, even though she was just wearing sweat-pants and a T-shirt with her hair pulled back in a ponytail. At first she looked confused. But when she saw Cosmo and me, she started to clue in that this performance was for her. She looked stunned, then embarrassed. Even in the fading evening light, I could see her face turn the same color as Cosmo's.

"I'm still ahead of all the chumps you never knew. And that's the truth."

The song ended. A few of the sidewalk gawkers clapped, and so did a handful of the women from Amanda's Stitch and Bitch group.

"What do you want?" Amanda asked, and I was bummed out because her voice carried the same edge of steel that it had on the last night we'd seen her.

"I just want to talk," said Cosmo.

She pursed her lips. Her Stitch and Bitch pals waited with bated breath. One of them nudged her encouragingly.

"Fine," she said, at last. "Come on up."

When we got to her door, the Stitch and Bitch ladies were just leaving. A few of them smiled at Cosmo on their way out, but more of them gave him dirty looks. I guessed they'd bitched about him more than once while they'd stitched.

We stepped inside. Amanda's apartment was tiny, but neat as a pin and full of really interesting stuff, like old movie posters and a collection of "I Love Lucy" plates that hung on the walls. She also had shelves full of female superhero action figures, like Wonder Woman and Batgirl.

"Nice apartment. Is that a Murphy bed?" I asked, pointing at a large slab of wood with a handle, in the middle of one wall.

"It is indeed," she said. Then she ruffled my hair. "It's good to see you, kiddo."

But when she turned to Cosmo, the smile disappeared and she crossed her arms over her chest. "You want to talk? Talk," she said.

Cosmo glanced at me. "You think you can give us some privacy, Ambrose?"

There was nowhere to go but the balcony or the bathroom, so I chose the balcony. I left the doors open a crack so I could hear everything.

"Amanda, you don't know how sorry I am," Cosmo was saying. "I just wish you'd give me a second chance."

"I'm going to tell you a story," Amanda said. "My last relationship, I was with the guy for three years. We were engaged, till I found out completely by accident that he'd been cheating on me, practically from the very beginning, with a string of different women. He told me they didn't count. I kicked him out that night and I haven't spoken to him since. So, as you can see, I'm not big on second chances."

"But I'm not like that –"

"You were the first man I liked enough to date since him. And I had my doubts about you, too. But then, you were a Big Brother, and you seemed so genuine. . . . You made me feel like a fool again, Cosmo. I refuse to be treated like a fool."

"I never thought of you as a fool, Amanda. I'm the fool. I thought, if I told you the truth, you wouldn't have even considered going out with me."

"You're probably right."

"I swear it won't happen again."

"But how do I know that?"

"You think I'd humiliate myself like that out there if I wasn't serious?"

I heard Amanda giggle, which was a good sign.

"I like you, Amanda. Very much."

"And I like you, too."

I peeked inside and saw Cosmo sit beside Amanda on her cherry red love seat. He took her hand. My heart felt lighter than it had in weeks.

"Tell you what," she said. "Start coming to Scrabble Club again, and we'll try to get reacquainted. But just as friends for now."

"Sounds fair."

"And, Ambrose, since I know you're listening, you can come inside now."

I thought about pretending I hadn't heard that, but there didn't seem to be much point, so in I came.

"I have something for you," said Amanda.

"What?"

She dug around for a piece of paper on a desk near the front door. "Everyone missed you at the club. Even Joan."

"I missed you guys, too."

"But if you want to come back, you need to get your mom to sign this." She found the piece of paper and handed it to me.

"What is it?"

"A consent form."

My heart sank. "What if she doesn't sign it?"

"Then you can't be in the club."

"You mean, you'd kick me out?"

"Put yourself in my shoes. I could get into a lot of trouble."

"Please don't give me the boot."

"I won't. Not as long as your mom signs this."

"It's not that simple," I said.

"Why not?"

"Yeah," said Cosmo, from the love seat. "What's the worst that could happen?"

The worst that could happen was that my mom would flip out a) that I'd been lying to her and b) that I'd been hanging out with an ex-con after promising I wouldn't. And that because of *a* and *b*, she'd do what she did in Edmonton when she got tired of her job, and in Regina when she got tired of Nana Ruth, and in Kelowna when she got fired from her job because she got drunk at a staff party and made wisecracks about the dean when he was standing right behind her, and in Calgary when my dad died and her work at the university went down the toilet because she was grieving, and they never did offer her a full-time position but instead let her go after two years: *She'd pack us up and move us to a whole new city and expect us both to start all over again.*

That was the worst that could happen.

But all I said to Cosmo and Amanda was "Fine. I'll give it a try."

20

V C N A I O D A E

dance, oven, voice, cove, naïve, cave, coin, invade

A V O I D A N C E

ut how's a guy supposed to begin in a situation like this? There's not just one lie, there's multiple lies, layered on top of each other like the fancy cakes that they sell at the Bon Ton on Broadway that Mom will never buy, partly because she's worried they might have peanuts in them and partly because she says they're empty calories (whatever that means).

I tried to work out the conversation ahead of time in my mind. *Mom, there's something I have to tell you. I've*

been going to the West Side Scrabble Club for a couple of
months now. Cosmo drives me. You know, Cosmo, the
ex-druggie? We've become good friends. I've even gone out
with him and his new friend, Amanda. Last week we went
rock climbing, which really isn't that dangerous. And you
know that night you saw him in his car with that girl?
Well, I was in the car too. We were just trying to beat you
home, ha-ha-ha.

Not in a million years was I going to say that.

On Sunday night, Mom and I played Scrabble and
listened to some of her CD's. I crushed her. The final
score was 302 to 125. She challenged about six different
words that I played, and each one was in the *Official
Scrabble Dictionary* (we used the regular Scrabble dictionary for our games, since Mom didn't even know I had the
Official Scrabble Tournament and Club World List).

She shook her head when we were done. "I didn't
think it was possible, but you've gotten even better. In
fact, you're not that much fun to play with anymore."
She smiled as she said this, but I could tell that part of
her meant it. And, inside, a part of me was pleased,
because I remembered what Mohammed had told me
on the first night I'd gone to the club, about his roommates refusing to play with him after a while. Maybe
this meant I wasn't just a kitchen player anymore.

And suddenly I knew how I could broach the subject
of the Scrabble Club. I simply needed to apply Scrabble

strategies. Scrabble wasn't just about having a good vocabulary; it was also about which letters you held on to and which you dumped.

More simply, I didn't have to tell my mom the entire truth. I could just use the parts I wanted to use and hold on to the rest.

"I do love Scrabble," I said, as she put the board away and poured herself another glass of wine.

"I know you do."

"It's something I'm good at," I continued, "something I take pride in." I knew this was a good thing to say. Mom was always wanting me to find something in my life that I could take pride in, and so far, in my twelve and three-quarter years, there'd been next to nothing, unless you counted the year I got a PARTICIPANT ribbon at the end of our school sports day in Regina.

"Where is this leading?" she asked.

"When we were on Broadway the other day," I continued, "I saw a notice on a hydro pole for the West Side Scrabble Club." This was not a lie, even if it had happened months ago. "I'd really like to join."

"A Scrabble Club? That sounds like fun."

"So, can I?"

"When is it?" She was dancing to the music – this one a CD by another Canadian guy named Luke Doucet – as she drank her wine, and, for a moment, I felt I was seeing her the way my dad must have seen her all those years ago, carefree and happy and maybe even fun.

"Wednesday nights at 7:00 P.M., at the West Side United Church."

"But that's up by the university."

"I can take the bus."

"By yourself?"

"Mom, I'm twelve and three-quarters. Thirteen in July."

She shook her head. "Sorry, Ambrose, there's no way I'm letting you take the bus by yourself, in the dark —"

"It's barely dark at seven, now that spring's here," I said.

"But what about later, when the club gets out?"

I almost suggested that she could pick me up on her way home, but then I remembered I couldn't let her find out that Cosmo was in the club, too.

"I'm sure someone would give me a lift."

She stopped dancing and turned off the music. "Ambrose, do I look like I'm nuts? Not in a million years would I let you get into a car with a perfect stranger."

"But they wouldn't be strangers after a couple of weeks."

"I'm sorry, but the answer is no."

I was desperate now. "What if I find someone else to drive me? Someone you know and trust?"

"And who would that be?"

"The Economopouloses? Maybe one of them would drive me."

"Mrs. Economopoulos doesn't even have her license. And have you seen Mr. Economopoulos drive? It's a miracle the man hasn't killed himself, or someone else."

"Then Cosmo." That just came flying out.

She gave me the stink-eye. "I truly am sorry, Ambrose. If I could go with you, if it was on the weekends, I'd take you in a heartbeat. But I would be a terrible mother if I agreed to this."

"Mom, please –"

"This discussion is over." She grabbed her glass of wine and walked into her bedroom and closed the door.

I stood thinking for a minute, then I pushed through the beads into my own bedroom and took the consent form out of my desk. I found a pen. Then, on the line after PARENT OR GUARDIAN SIGNATURE, I wrote in my best handwriting: *Irene Bukowski.*

Cosmo and I returned to the Scrabble Club that Wednesday. He didn't ask about my mom on the drive up, and I was grateful. We talked mostly about the weather, which I've noticed Vancouverites like to do.

But for the first time since we started going to the Scrabble Club, I felt kind of guilty. At least before, I'd had the excuse that Mom had never said I couldn't go because I'd never told her. Now I knew exactly where she stood, and I was one hundred percent going against her wishes.

My feelings were quickly forgotten, though, as soon as we stepped into the Sunday school room.

"Welcome back," said Mohammed, and he handed me a word list he'd printed out especially for me.

"We thought we'd lost you," said a woman named Beth.

It was a nice feeling to know we'd been missed, even if we hadn't been gone that long. Even Joan and I were getting along better, ever since I'd told her about my peanut allergy and she'd told me about her lactose intolerance.

"How are you feeling tonight, Joan?" I asked, as we set up the boards and counted tiles.

"Terrible. I had a Greek salad at lunch and they swore up and down that the feta was made from goat's milk, but the way my tummy's been feeling, I just know it was cow's. I've been burbly and gaseous for hours."

And she proved it by letting off a long fart, so I was relieved when I found out that we had six beginners present and I wouldn't be playing Joan.

Once we'd all sat down in our little kid chairs, Amanda made the announcements. "If anyone has seen Susan's timer, please let her know. She hasn't been able to find it since last week. And Larry went down to the tournament in Portland and improved his rating by one hundred points, winning ten out of fourteen games. His rating is now 1767 – congratulations, Larry!" Everyone applauded and Larry, in his stained sweatpants, took a bow. "And of course our most exciting news is that our annual West Side Scrabble Club tournament is only three weeks away. It's on Saturday, May 14th. We'll be playing eight games. Players need to be there by eight-thirty in the morning and we hope to wrap up by six. I've received over seventy-five entry forms already. We have people coming from as far as Boston, Massachusetts, and Sacramento, California. If you haven't entered yet but would still like to, time's running out. We need your applications and your checks in by this Saturday, at the latest."

Then it was time to play. In spite of all my mixed feelings about Mom, I got sucked right into it again. For the first time, I won all three of my games. Even Cosmo managed to win two out of three.

So we were both floating a bit when Amanda approached us afterward. "Did you tell your mom about the club?" she asked.

"Yes," I said, which, technically speaking, wasn't a lie.

"And?"

"And, it's fine." Technically speaking, that was a lie. "Did you bring the consent form?"

I nodded and handed it to her. She looked at it and so did Cosmo and, suddenly, I felt kind of sweaty in my armpits.

But all she said was "Well, that's fantastic. Especially since I think you should enter the tournament."

"Really?"

"You're ready, Ambrose. Cosmo, I think you should enter, too. You're both getting better. Until you play in a tournament, you can't get a ranking. If you want to get more serious about your playing, this is your next step. And it's also a heck of a lot of fun." She handed us both application forms, but when Cosmo tried to give her a quick kiss good night on the lips, she turned her face so it landed on her cheek instead.

On the drive home, Cosmo said, "You forged her signature, didn't you?"

I didn't say anything.

"Ambrose."

"I'm not telling you anything," I blurted. "You've promised to be Mr. Honesty, haven't you? You'll feel all morally obligated to tell Amanda."

"I wouldn't do that."

I looked out the window, suddenly wishing I was home and that my mom was there and that we could just curl up on the couch and watch an old movie, like we used to once in a while before she'd had to switch to teaching nights.

"I tried to tell her. But there were so many parts I couldn't say."

"Like that you and I go together."

I didn't answer.

"She doesn't like me."

"No, she doesn't," I said. "But all she knows about you is that you're an ex-con and a drug addict. You can't totally blame her."

"But if she got to know me. . . ."

"It wouldn't matter. She wouldn't trust you: Are you just being nice because you're a pedophile and you're going to kidnap me; are you just being nice because you want me to start selling drugs for you; are you just being nice so I'll feel too guilty to tell when you molest me?"

"Holy sh—"

"It's how her mind works. I told her I could take the bus to the Scrabble Club, but all she thinks about is a stranger getting off the bus and following me. Or she imagines a creepy guy befriending me, then killing me. Or she pictures me getting hit by a car when I cross a busy street without her."

"Those are some very dark thoughts."

"I know. But maybe we'd have them, too, if we lost someone the way she lost my dad. Everything's normal in the morning – he's there patting her stomach and kissing her good-bye – and then *boom*. He's dead because of a time bomb in his brain."

We were both pretty quiet after that. When we got out of the car at home, Cosmo held up the entry forms Amanda had given us. "You gonna enter?"

I shook my head. "I'd like to. But it's a Saturday. My mom doesn't work. Besides, it costs forty bucks."

"Well, if you change your mind, I can spot you the entrance fee. It looks like I'm going to pick up a few more shifts at the construction sight."

"That's good news." Then, because I had to ask, "Have you tried to buy drugs again?"

He shook his head. "No, I haven't. Have you ditched your purple pants yet?"

"Not gonna happen," I replied.

We said good night. Cosmo started up the front steps while I headed around the side of the house. Suddenly I heard him swear loudly, one of the ten uses of the "f" word in the *Official Scrabble Tournament and Club Word List*.

I ran up to the porch. He stood, looking through the living room window. Right through the living room window. Because the glass, aside from a few shards, was no longer there.

Someone had thrown a rock right through it.

21

L C M E A I R

cream, clear, real, mice, éclair, lime, mile, meal, realm

MIRACLE

osmo didn't want me to come in with him, but he also didn't want me to call the cops, so I stood outside, feeling shivery and numb and scared.

After a few minutes, he told me it was okay to come in.

"Nothing seems to be missing," he said.

"It was a message, wasn't it?" I told him. "You owe me."

"No," he said. "It was kids. A random prank."

"But —"

"Did you hear what I said?"

"Yeah. Got it." And I did. He was telling me that it was better for him — better for both of us — if that's what everyone else who lived here thought this was.

"How horrible, what happened to the Economopouloses," my mom said, as we walked over to Cypress Elementary the next day. It was a beautiful warm April afternoon, and it was even more special because it came after three days of rain. The warm sun on the wet grass and the trees and the millions of colorful flowers that now bloomed all over the place made everything smell delicious.

"Dumb teenagers," I said.

"I picked this neighborhood because it was supposed to be safe. Then we wind up with an ex-con upstairs, and now this. . . ."

"Mom. It *is* safe."

I logged on to my cyber-teacher and, as usual, Mr. Acheson stopped by to say hello. He was all dressed up in a navy blue suit that I hadn't seen before and he looked like he'd lost some weight. He and my mother wandered off to talk about who knows what while I got my work done. As usual, I didn't budge from the lab until my mom returned; I'd learned my lesson about leaving the school solo. She was a few minutes late, again. While I waited, I thought I caught a glimpse of Troy walking past, and I wondered what poor sucker the Three Stooges had chosen to pick on, now that I was gone.

Like I said, it was just a routine day. That is, until we got home. Because that's when a miracle happened. A minor miracle, but still, one of those perfect little moments that make you think there really is a Higher Being up there, and that for one random moment, he's watching over you and no one else.

Mom was listening to music while she made one of her tuna casseroles, so I'd have something to eat once she left for work. I was reading *Inkspell,* the sequel to *Inkheart.*

Mom put the casserole into the oven, then she turned to me. "Ambrose, we need to talk."

"About what?"

"Put your book down."

She turned off the music and sat beside me on the couch. I put my book down and looked at her. She sounded serious, and she looked serious, too. My stomach started to do somersaults. I was sure I was busted. She must have found out Cosmo and I were spending time together.

"You know that I will never love any man the way I loved your father," she began.

"Yeah."

"And you know that my first priority, forever and always, is you, Ambrose. You're the most important person in my life, period."

"I do know that." And suddenly I felt a wave of panic. She was going to tell me she had six months to live. "Mom, is something wrong? Are you sick?"

She laughed and said, "Oh, God, no, nothing like that." She took a deep breath and continued, "I've been asked on a date."

"A date?"

"Well, it's not really a date, it's a one-day cooking class."

"Who asked you?"

"Bob. Mr. Acheson."

"You're kidding me." But I knew she wasn't. All those times he'd "casually" dropped by now made perfect sense. Still, it was hard to imagine Mr. Acheson, with his nose hairs and his wacky ties and his receding hairline, dating anyone, let alone my mom.

"It's a funny story, actually," Mom continued, twirling a piece of hair on her finger – a sure sign she was nervous. "He won a contest. He entered his name in a draw at a bookstore, and he won two tickets to an all-day Italian cooking course at Barbara Jo's Books to Cooks two Saturdays from now. So, in some ways, it's not really a date, we're just . . . taking a course together, and I thought, well, it wouldn't hurt for me to learn a few more skills in the kitchen. . . ."

She looked at me, concerned, because I was dead quiet. I was quiet partly because I just couldn't picture my mom with Mr. Acheson, but mostly because I was thinking that the Scrabble tournament was two Saturdays from now. She could go to her cooking course. I could play in the tournament.

"Ambrose, if you don't want me to go, just say so. I'll call him and tell him no. In fact, I should probably call and tell him no anyway –"

"No!" I shouted, startling her. "I mean . . . of course you should go. You should go on dates. You're not bad looking for someone your age."

"*Gee*, thanks," she said.

"You're welcome. Just – don't look in his nose. He has lots of nose hairs."

"Really? I hadn't noticed. Actually, I think he's kind of cute."

I almost fake-barfed, but I stopped myself.

"You're honestly sure you're okay with this?"

"I'm sure. Go."

She smiled, relieved.

And so did I.

Later that afternoon, I was on a cloud when Mom went to work. I wanted to run upstairs and tell Cosmo the good news, but I remembered he had an NA meeting after work. The Economopouloses were out, too, because I couldn't hear their footsteps or their Greek music upstairs.

So I warmed up some tuna casserole and ate it, then I practiced my blocks and my punches to a Bryan Adams CD. When I was done, I got out some of the word lists Mohammed had printed up for me and put on the TV for company.

At about eight o'clock, there was a knock on the door.

It was dark outside, and I could just see a figure through the gauze curtain on the window. Our outdoor light had burned out, so I couldn't flip it on for a better look. I figured it was Cosmo, home from his meeting. But when I threw open the door, it wasn't Cosmo.

It was Silvio.

You know that expression, "My heart leapt into my throat"? Well, that's what mine did. He was even scarier looking up close and he was standing under our outside light. His skin was kind of gray and his teeth were all crooked and yellow.

"Hey. Remember me?" he said. He smiled, but it wasn't friendly.

"Sh-should I?" I squeaked.

"I'm your uncle Cosmo's friend."

"Oh, yeah. *Um,* he's not home right now." I tried

to close the door, but he held out one powerful arm to stop it.

"You're not really his nephew, are you?"

"I – what are you talking about?"

"You think I'm an idiot?"

"No." My stomach felt queasy. I was afraid I might have a diarrhea poo, right there in front of him, right in my pants. All I could think about was that he could kill me with his bare hands and my mom would find the body when she came home from work. All her over-protective theories would be proved right, and she'd be left truly alone in the world. It was enough to make me want to cry.

"Pass a message on to your 'uncle' for me, will you?"

I nodded.

"Tell him his buddy Silvio dropped by tonight. And I want what he owes me."

"He's working on it, I swear, he told me –"

"You tell him fifty bucks here and fifty bucks there doesn't cut it. I want my money. Paid in full. Or else."

"Or else what?" I couldn't help asking.

He didn't answer that. He just said, "Think you can manage that?"

I nodded.

"Great. Then have a nice evening. And lock the door behind me. Hasn't your mother warned you not to open the door to strangers?" He laughed like he thought this was really funny and sauntered away.

I slammed the door and locked it and dragged a heavy chair in front of it. I'd have to remember to remove the chair before Mom got home, which meant I wouldn't be able to go to bed before then.

But that wouldn't be a problem. No way would I be sleeping a wink tonight.

22

P T H R U I M T A N

truth, pith, train, trip, mirth, ruin, truant

T R I U M P H A N T

N ow that the weather was getting nicer and the days longer, the Economopouloses started doing a lot more barbecuing. I would wander into the backyard whenever I smelled meat cooking, and they'd always invite me to join them. I never said no.

One night, Amanda came over. She and Cosmo were taking it slow, but she'd agreed to his invitation for dinner and to meet his family. She arrived at the door wearing a moss green sweater that was made of the softest wool in the world. I know because I got to touch it when she gave me a hug hello.

Cosmo blushed as he brought her into the living room and introduced her. "Ma, Pop, this is Amanda Svecova. She's . . ." He searched for the right word. ". . . a friend."

Mr. and Mrs. E were very polite, but they spoke a lot in Greek to Cosmo. Finally Cosmo laughed and said in English, "You're right, she isn't Greek."

Mrs. E punched Cosmo in the arm, embarrassed that he'd translated, but Amanda just smiled. "I'm half Czech, half Irish from way back when, but mostly I'm Canadian."

After that, things settled down and Amanda scored bonus points with Mr. E when she told him that "The Mercer Report" was one of her favorite shows on TV, because it was one of Mr. E's favorites, too.

"That Rick, he should run for prime minister," Mr. E said, in remarkably good English. "Him or the Brent Butt from 'Corner Gas.'"

She scored points with Mrs. E, too, when she asked for seconds. "I like that," Mrs. E whispered to me. "A girl who's not afraid to eat."

I wanted to help Cosmo and Amanda in any way I could, so I said, "You're right. She eats like a pig."

After supper, Amanda insisted on helping Mrs. E with the dishes. Cosmo, Mr. E, and I settled into our seats in the living room and turned on a soccer game on TV. But a minute later, Amanda marched back in and said, "Cosmo? Ambrose? Did I mention you're drying?"

We groaned, but we got up and helped. Cosmo kept flicking his dish towel at Amanda and Mrs. E. They yelled at him to stop, but they were laughing too.

When we were done, Amanda went to her car. She came back with her Scrabble board and set it up on the dining room table. "Okay, Ambrose," she said. "You're going to play a game against me."

She stopped a lot as we played. "See how I just laid tiles on a triple word score? You could have prevented me from doing that," she said, and she showed me how. She also showed me how to keep track of what tiles were left in the bag, so I could roughly guess what letters my opponent had and how I could make multiple words in just one turn. Cosmo watched, and even Mr. and Mrs. E wandered in and out to see how we were doing.

Then she tried to teach me some relaxation techniques. "In case you ever start to panic," she said. "It happens to the best of us."

She taught me how to take a deep breath in, then a deep breath out, to calm my nerves. "Then there's positive imaging," she said. "If you get into a tight spot, imagine something that makes you really calm and content. Go on, try it."

So I did. I had a hard time coming up with something at first. Then I thought of my dad. His image made me feel calm and content, but it also made me sad and lonely. I'd have to work on the positive imaging.

I thought about telling Cosmo about my visit from Silvio, but there was never a good time, and I just didn't see the point. I knew he was working on paying Silvio back, and I knew he didn't want to borrow money from his parents, so why stress him out even more? It wasn't like there was much else he could do about it. Nothing legal, anyway.

The weeks passed and suddenly it was the night before the tournament. My mind was full of words and my stomach was doing somersaults (*maestros, masseurs, molasses, amulets, armless, assumes, ass*). It was impossible to sleep. Finally, after tossing and turning till about three o'clock in the morning, I got up to grab a glass of water. My mom was sitting on the couch.

"Mom?"

"What are you doing up?"

"Couldn't sleep."

"Me, neither."

I sat beside her. She was looking through our favorite photo album, the one with all the pictures of Dad. She'd taken almost all of them herself.

"I don't think I should go to the cooking class," she said.

My heart sank. "Why?"

"I think I'll call Bob and cancel."

"You can't do that!" I must've said it a bit too loud because she looked at me funny. But then I figured it out. She couldn't sleep. She was staring at photos of Dad. "Mom, Dad wouldn't mind."

She just turned the page.

"He's been dead almost thirteen years. And everything you've ever told me about him . . . he was a great guy."

"He really was, Ambrose."

"Then he'd want you to move on."

"I'm hardly 'moving on.' It's just a cooking class."

"Exactly. It's just a cooking class. Besides, you can't cancel now. Mr. Acheson would never find someone else."

She sighed. "You're right. I'll go. As long as you promise me you're truly okay with it."

"Mom. I am truly okay with it."

Which was mostly true.

Mom was supposed to leave by eight o'clock in the morning. Cosmo and I were going to meet in his drive- way as soon as she'd left. At 8:05 she stepped out of her bedroom, dressed in jeans and a white T-shirt. I tried not to look anxious as she pulled on her brown suede jacket.

"How do I look?" she asked. Her brow was furrowed as she checked herself out in the full-length mirror that hung by our apartment entrance.

"You look great," I said. "Casual, but great."

She nodded. "You're right. It's too casual."

"That's not what I meant –"

But she was already back in her bedroom, changing. I paced the living room, staring at the clock. At 8:13 she emerged again, this time in a black skirt, gray blouse, and high heels.

"Well?"

"Perfect. Beautiful. Elegant," I said hastily. "Now get going, or you're going to be late."

"You're right," she said. "It's too elegant."

Oh, man. She disappeared back into her room.

This time I took the opportunity to dash outside to the driveway, where Cosmo stood waiting. "What's taking you so long?" he demanded.

"My mom," I replied. "She's having a fashion crisis. Don't leave without me."

"Hurry!" he shouted after me, as I raced back into our apartment, just in time to see Mom emerge from her bedroom, this time in a blue skirt and a white blouse.

"Perfect!" I declared. "As Goldilocks would say, it's 'just right.'"

This was the correct thing to say, I guess, because her face relaxed into a smile. "Would you look at the time," she said. I wanted to shout that I *was* looking at the time, that I knew all too well that it was now 8:28. She grabbed her purse.

"Okay, bye, have fun," I said.

"You have Bob's cell phone number?"

"Yes."

"You can check in with me anytime."

"I know."

"If you go out, stick to the neighborhood."

"Yes."

"And don't cross any busy roads."

"Mom! I know. We've been through all of this."

"Fine," she said. "The class goes till six. I'll see you by six-thirty or seven."

And then, at 8:33 precisely, she left.

I waited till she was safely out of sight, then I ran to the driveway. Cosmo and I raced to the Kitsilano Community Centre, which was where the tournament was being held because the West Side United Church was too small to fit everyone.

"What have I told you about the purple pants?" Cosmo asked, eyeing my clothes as we drove through the side streets.

"They're my lucky pants," I said. I was wearing a bright red-hooded sweatshirt on top that said I'M FEELING LUCKY on the front, another primo garage-sale find. On my feet were my Ikes. I thought I looked pretty good.

"Well, you certainly are colorful, I'll give you that," he said.

"You're letting your tattoo show," I replied, looking at his short-sleeved T-shirt.

"I'm hoping it'll intimidate some of my opponents. I need all the help I can get."

When we parked on a tree-lined street near the center, he hauled a big basket out of the trunk.

"What's that?"

"A picnic lunch. I made it," he said proudly. "I'm hoping Amanda will join us."

We started walking to the community center, which, between its buildings and its grounds, took up two full city blocks. It was a gorgeous, warm, sunny May day, and the adjoining sports fields were full of teams playing soccer and baseball.

The place was just as busy inside, and I realized most of the people were heading into the gym Amanda had rented for the tournament.

"How many people are here?" I asked Amanda, when we saw her at the door.

"At last count, we had close to a hundred entries,"

she replied. "But enough chitchat, you'd better get a move on. Your first game starts in five minutes."

I ran to the bathroom and had a diarrhea poo.

Five minutes later I hurried into the gymnasium. It was full of row upon row of tables and chairs. Close to a hundred Scrabble players from across North America were settling into the chairs, and many of them were setting up their own special Scrabble boards. Some were custom-made and some, Amanda told me later, were even homemade. I saw a few people wearing earplugs to block out extra noise. One guy had a sock monkey propped up beside him on the table, which I guessed was his good luck charm, sort of like my purple pants.

I checked the play lists and found my seat across from a little old lady with blue-white hair. Her name was Betsy and she wore a dress with butterflies all over it. She looked a bit like Nana Ruth. Amanda had told me that since I wasn't ranked yet, I'd play with other unranked players for the first two games. After that, the computer would decide who I'd play with in my division, trying to match me to people with similar scores.

I asked Betsy where she was from.

"Comox" was all she said, then it was time to choose our tiles. Betsy drew an "A," so she started. She looked like a kitchen player, and I relaxed a little, knowing I would have an easy opponent my first game of the day.

But when her first word was "ANTHEMS," for a double word score, a double letter score, and a bingo of an extra fifty points for using all her letters, I knew that I was in trouble.

"Seventy-six points," she said, hitting her clock. Then she cackled loudly. "Try beating that, midget."

Okay. She was nothing like Nana Ruth.

I looked at my tiles, and that's when I started to panic: "EIOIXKM." All I could come up with were dinky words, like "HEM" from her "H," or "MIME" from her "M." My clock was ticking. I knew there must be other words, but I couldn't see them. Across from me, Betsy was clicking her false teeth and making funny noises with her throat, and I was pretty sure she was doing it on purpose. I could feel my stomach lurch again and I felt like I needed another poo and this was only one minute into the first game.

Then I remembered what Amanda had taught me, about breathing and positive imaging. I figured it was worth a shot. I started breathing in slowly and exhaling slowly. In my mind I pictured a babbling brook, but that was too hokey, so I tried to picture Amanda without her top on, which I know was kind of sinful (especially since Cosmo liked her), but it made me feel much better and kind of warm all over, and I didn't even hear Betsy's teeth anymore. After what felt like three minutes, but was really only thirty seconds, I opened my eyes and looked at my letters. The answer was right there in front of me. Calmly I picked up my "E" and my "X" and placed them in front of "ANTHEMS," with the "E" on the triple word score to create "EXANTHEMS."

"Sixty-three," I said, and hit the button on the clock.

She snorted. "I challenge."

So we walked over to the nearest "Word Judge" computer and she punched in the word. I was feeling pretty pleased because I knew it was good, and it was. It was the plural for "a skin eruption."

Betsy lost her turn, and boy, was she miffed. She was miffed when, later in the game, I got the "Q" tile and played "QUIT" and "QI" in one turn, getting the points for the "Q" on a double letter score twice. She was miffed when I played "ORACH" and she challenged again and lost another turn. Meanwhile, she placed a lot of good words, too: bingoing again with "OPOSSUMS" and "URETHANE" and building "AA" and "SH" when she laid down "POTASH."

But I won – 348 to 322.

Betsy wasn't happy. I reached across the table to shake her hand, but she ignored that and said, "Since when do they let smartass kids into these tournaments anyway?" Then she stormed away as fast as her walker would let her, which wasn't very fast.

Across the room, Cosmo, who'd just finished his first game, gave me an inquiring look. I gave him the thumbs-up. He gave me the thumbs-down, but as usual, he didn't seem upset that he'd lost his first game. I noticed that a lot of the players spent any time left over after a game to analyze it, discussing words they'd played and words they should have played. Aside from the odd person like Betsy, it was a pretty friendly atmosphere.

Game Two I played against a tall wiry guy with bad skin, whose name was Kamal. A fedora was perched on his head. He played really well, but he took a long time, so even though his score was higher than mine at the end, he had forty points taken off for going four minutes over. I won by six points. Game Three I played against a friendly, chatty lady about my mom's age, with beautiful dark skin and thick black hair. She laughed a lot and banged her forehead with the palm of her hand whenever she made a bad play, which was kind of often. I beat her easily, 318 to 251. Game Four I played against a shy man who couldn't even make eye contact, and, to be honest, he had really bad breath. He was from Seattle, Washington, and he wore a faded, rumpled two-piece gray suit. He crushed me 357 to 275.

Still, it had been a great morning. I'd won three out of my four games. When Cosmo heard the news, he thumped me so hard on the back, I almost fell over. He'd won one of his four, but he didn't seem to care. In fact, he was in a great mood because Amanda had agreed to have lunch with us.

It was a beautiful day. Cosmo had packed us a big picnic lunch – cold fried chicken, dolmades (that he confessed his mom had made), a baguette, cheese, and some huge homemade cookies (also made by Mrs. E). A lot of players had questions for Amanda, so I took the picnic basket from Cosmo, who was waiting patiently for her.

"I'll find us a spot in the shade," I said. Because I burn easily, I put up the hood on my red sweatshirt as I walked away. On the playing fields, games were breaking up and new teams were arriving.

I found us a perfect spot under a big maple tree. Just as I was about to put the basket down, I heard, "Look, it's Little Red Riding Hood on her way to Granny's house."

I knew that voice. And that voice made me freeze.

Sure enough, when I mustered up the courage to unfreeze and turn around, I saw Troy jogging toward me. Mike and Josh weren't far behind. They were all in their soccer uniforms and, from the large sweat stains on their shirts, I knew they'd just finished a game.

"Guys. Long time no see."

"Look at him," said Troy, talking about me in the third person. "He's still a total fag, prancing around with a picnic basket."

"It's almost as bad as his hot pink fanny pack," Mike added.

"It's not my picnic basket. It's a friend's."

"*Ooh*, a friend's. Is he another homo like you?" Josh said, and they all cracked up.

"I'm not gay. Although I have nothing against people who are –"

This time, Josh shoved me first.

"Okay, listen," I said, trying to reason with them. "I never should have pretended you guys were my friends. It was stupid. But you did try to kill me, so why don't we say we're even and call it quits –"

Mike shoved me next and I almost fell over the picnic basket.

"Don't," I said.

"Hey, Josh, open the picnic basket," said Troy. "Let's see what Hambrose and his faggot friend are having for lunch."

"Yeah, I'm starving," Mike said.

Josh made a grab for the picnic basket, and suddenly one of the moves Cosmo taught me flashed before my eyes. I blocked Josh's arm with my own.

"Leave it alone," I said. "My friend put a lot of work into that."

"Screw you," Josh said, and he tried to grab the basket with his other hand, but I blocked that one, too.

Then Mike and Troy made a move for the basket. I blocked it with my body and went into what I hoped looked like some kind of karate pose. I tried to make a convincing sound effect to go with it, like *"Heee-yaaaa!"* Then I picked up the closest weapon I could find, which was the baguette.

Troy made a grab for the bread, but I just started swinging it like I was some kind of ninja, complete with a whole pile of sounds, like *"Waaaaaaaaaaaaaaaa,"* and *"Hiiiiiiiiiiiiiiiiiiiiiiiii."* They covered their heads and I jabbed them with the loaf. The most amazing part of it was, I wasn't scared. Cosmo's self-defense lessons had actually helped. I just had to believe in myself.

Then Troy shouted, "You're crazy," and he grabbed the baguette out of my hand and snapped it neatly in two. He threw the bread onto the ground and then he punched me in the stomach, hard.

Okay, so believing in myself isn't enough, I thought, as he came at me again. But this time another one of Cosmo's moves popped into my head and before Troy could punch me, I brought my arm back, just like Cosmo had taught me. With all the force and energy I could muster, I swung my fist forward.

And my fist connected.

With Troy's nose.

It made quite a satisfying sound.

"You turd!" Troy shouted, as he grabbed his nose in pain. I saw that it was bleeding.

I won't lie. It felt pretty good – no, it felt awesome – to see him standing there with a bloody nose, after all the grief he'd caused me. But it only felt good for a moment because it was still three against one. I figured I was officially a dead man.

But I must've really messed up Troy, because the next thing I knew, he started backing away. Mike and Josh followed him. I couldn't believe it. I'd single-handedly scared the Three Stooges into backing down. I couldn't resist shouting after them, "And from now on, leave me the hell alone!"

I picked up the two baguette halves and brushed them off, then I started to laugh.

"What's so funny?" I turned to see Cosmo, walking toward me.

"You'll never guess what happened," I said. "I scared off the Three Stooges with a baguette and a punch in the nose."

Cosmo smiled. "Good for you, buddy. And three against one."

"Your self-defense lessons really worked, Cosmo. I

blocked some of their moves, and my swing, when I hit him – I wish you could've seen it."

Then Amanda joined us. I guess she could see I was walking on a cloud because she asked, "What's all the excitement?"

"Our lunch was in peril and I saved it," I told her, then I repeated the entire play-by-play action for them both. Amanda wasn't happy that I'd punched a guy in the nose, but that was okay. I didn't really expect a woman, especially a woman who didn't know the Three Stooges, to understand.

But Cosmo understood, I could tell. He kept getting me to show him my swing during lunch.

Which was delicious. The mental exertion of the tournament, combined with the physical exertion of the fight, had made me ravenous. Four pieces of chicken, two cartons of milk, five pieces of bread with cheese, and three cookies later, I lay back on the grass and belched.

It wasn't until we were heading back inside that it dawned on me why Troy and his friends had really run away.

They'd seen Cosmo coming. It was him they were afraid of, not me or my baguette or my right hook. I suddenly wondered if Cosmo had been watching the whole time, waiting to see if I needed him to step in and save me.

But even if he had been, it was okay. Because I'd stood up to the Three Stooges. I hadn't been scared.

And best of all, I'd thrown a pretty good punch.

The afternoon went really well. I won my first two games, lost my third, and won my fourth (against Joan, but since we shared food issues, she didn't seem to mind).

I'd won six out of eight games. Cosmo had won two out of eight, but he was grinning and laughing and having a ball. I felt absolutely wiped, like I would pass out right there and then on the cool gym floor. But we couldn't leave yet; Amanda still had to give out the prizes.

There were four divisions. The top three players in each division won cash prizes. The biggest cash prize was five hundred dollars, given to the winner in division one – Freddy Wong, a Scrabble legend from San Francisco. Larry Schell, from our very own West Side Scrabble Club, wearing the same stained sweatpants and sandals without socks, came in second and won three hundred bucks.

Amanda also gave out some funny awards, like the "Hardest Day" award to the player who'd lost the most, and the "Highest Scoring Non-Bingo Word" award.

When I thought she was finished, I stood up to stretch my legs. But she wasn't.

"I also have a couple of special prizes to give out," she said. "The first one is for the 'Most Promising Newcomer.' And I think everyone in the West Side Scrabble Club will agree when I say that this award goes most deservedly to Ambrose Bukowski, age twelve and three-quarters."

The West Side Scrabble Club members all started to clap loudly. Me, I didn't do anything; I stood frozen to the spot. Joan, who was sitting beside me, gave me a friendly nudge, and Cosmo whistled through his fingers from across the gym.

I barely remember the long walk up to Amanda at the front. It felt like I was trudging through molasses, or mud, and my legs were numb and there was a ringing in my ears. She handed me a trophy. It had a wooden base, on which sat a little silver cup. A brass plaque read MOST PROMISING NEWCOMER, VANCOUVER SCRABBLE TOURNAMENT, AMBROSE BUKOWSKI. The print was small so they could fit it all onto the plaque.

I had never won anything in my entire life. It felt like a great big rubber ball was rising up in my throat.

"Thank you," I whispered. Then I ran from the gym, my legs working just fine again. I dashed into the men's washroom and locked myself into a stall and burst into tears.

23

SWEDCRE

crews, weds, creed, sewed, weeds, drew, dew

SCREWED

his was the best day of my life," I blubbered, as Amanda, Cosmo, and I left the community center just after six.

"Well, you sure have a funny way of showing it," Cosmo laughed. But he put his arm around me and patted my shoulder.

We arrived at Cosmo's car. "Can I offer you a lift?" he asked Amanda.

"Actually, some of us are going to Milestone's," she said.

I could tell Cosmo was trying not to look disappointed. "Oh. Okay."

"But we could all go," she continued.

Cosmo's frown turned upside down. "I'd like that," he replied.

I glanced at my watch. Mom's cooking course ended at six and it was already five minutes to. "I think I'll take a pass," I said. "I'm pretty tired."

They drove me home. "Want us to come in?" asked Amanda. "I'd like to meet your mom. It's a shame she couldn't make it to the tournament today."

"You can't meet her," I said. "She isn't home yet." Which wasn't a lie.

Cosmo let me out of the backseat. "You did amazing today, buddy. You should be very proud."

"You're going to wind up with a rating of close to four hundred," Amanda said. "It may not sound like much, compared to the experts, but for your first one-day tournament, it's pretty darn good."

I hopped out of the car clutching my trophy and waved as they drove away, feeling a twinge of sadness that I couldn't join them to celebrate.

And that's when another miracle happened, the second one in less than two weeks. My cell phone rang.

"Hello?"

"Ambrose?" It was my mom. "I tried the house, but you weren't there."

"No, I'm just out front. I went for a little walk."

"You didn't talk to any strangers, I hope."

"No, Mom."

"Listen . . . we've finished the cooking course, but Bob was wondering if I'd like to go out for a quick bite to eat. Italian, of course, *ha-ha*. But I said I'd have to check with you first. If you'd rather I didn't –"

"Go. Of course you should go," I said, and I really meant it for her too, not just for me. "When will you be home?"

"By ten at the latest. I promise."

"Okay," I said, and I was already running down the street.

"You're sure you're fine with this?"

"Positive."

"Why do you sound out of breath all of a sudden?"

"I'm doing jumping jacks," I said, because it was the first thing that came into my mind.

I heard her laugh on the other end of the line. "Okay, sweetheart. Love you."

"Love you, too."

I hung up and ran like the wind in my Ikes, all the way down to Milestone's at Bayswater and 4th Avenue, thinking that this was the second time in two weeks that a Higher Power had been watching over me.

I ran so fast that Cosmo and Amanda were just walking through the front door when I arrived.

The best day of my life turned into the best night of my life. There were about twelve of us in all. Mohammed and Joan and Larry were there from our club. Freddy Wong, the champion, showed up. A bunch of the other out-of-towners came, too. We got the waiters to put a bunch of tables together, and I sat in between Cosmo and Mohammed and right across from Freddy, which was a real honor. Freddy told us all a bunch of stories about being at the World Scrabble Championships two years earlier, where he'd placed fifteenth out of about a hundred top players. He also gave me tips on word study techniques, which I thought was pretty cool of him. He seemed like a great down-to-earth guy, and he even signed my napkin when I asked.

When our waitress approached, I couldn't help but notice that she had even bigger boobs than Amanda. "For the young gentleman?" she said, when it was my turn to order.

"I'll just have water," I replied.

Cosmo turned to me. "Aren't you hungry?"

"I don't have any money," I whispered to him.

"No worries. Buy whatever you want. It's on me."

"But you can't afford –"

"I forgot to tell you. I got called into the foreman's office yesterday," he said. "Starting Monday, I have full-time work."

"That's awesome!" I said, then I grabbed a menu and gave it a quick scan. After I gave our waitress the lowdown about my peanut allergy, I ordered a huge plate of fettuccine Alfredo and a Roy Rogers – some kind of fancy cocktail minus the booze.

Around me everyone was laughing and talking and analyzing the plays they'd made that day, and not just with each other, but with me too. It was the strangest yet best feeling in the world to realize that I was a part of this. And as I sat there sipping my second Roy Rogers, it dawned on me that this was what it was like to have friends. People who liked you for you. People you didn't have to try to impress. And even though they were all older than me and some of them were much older than me, it didn't matter. Suddenly I felt kind of emotional again. I guess Cosmo noticed because he leaned in and asked if I was okay, and I told him, with total honesty, "I'm fantastic."

Then I went to the bathroom because I really needed to pee after my second Roy Rogers. When I returned, one of the out-of-town players was sitting in my seat, so I sat in hers, which put me beside Larry Schell. I had never sat close to Larry before since he was in the expert division, so it was the first time I noticed that he smelled, like a mix of old socks and rancid butter. I guess he was really enjoying his food because he made a *mmmmm* sound while he chewed.

I decided I should try to make small talk, so I said, "When did you start playing Scrabble, Larry?"

"I played with Mother, growing up." It was hard to hear Larry because he kind of mumbled, but fortunately my hearing was twenty-twenty.

"Hey, me too. I mean, I'm still growing up. But I play with my mom."

He nodded. "My sister would go to the parties, and I'd stay home with Mother and play. I wasn't invited to the parties. But that was okay."

I suddenly had a very clear picture of Larry as a kid. I could see him being picked on and being called names, like Larry Smells.

"And who do you play with now?" I asked politely.

"Mother. And the West Side Scrabble Club, once a week. But Mother, mostly. I can't work because I have a lot of, *um*, health issues. So I still live at home."

"Oh," I said. Larry must have been at least forty.

"Scrabble's my life. I play Scrabble and, when I'm not playing, I study words. Or watch TV. I love TV. Especially 'CSI.'"

Maybe it was mean, but suddenly I didn't want to talk to Larry anymore. I thought about what Cosmo had told me, about the paths we choose in life, and how it's easy to make a wrong turn. When I looked at Larry, I got this uneasy feeling that if I made a wrong turn, I could wind up just like him.

These were pretty deep thoughts and I wasn't in a deep mood, so when the out-of-town lady got up to use the bathroom, I excused myself and slipped back in beside Cosmo. Amanda sat to his left, and when I bent down to pick up my napkin, I saw that they were holding hands under the table.

For dessert, I had a big piece of apple pie à la mode, brought to me by our waitress, who assured me it had been made in a peanut-free bakery.

"Most promising newcomer, huh?" she said, when she saw my trophy. "I bet a lot of girls at your school say that about you, too," and she gave me a dazzling smile.

"That they do, but I tell them I only have eyes for you, Sandy," I replied, quickly looking at the name tag on her big boobs.

After she'd walked away, Cosmo and Mohammed burst out laughing. "Ambrose, you are going to be a lady-killer," Cosmo said.

Mohammed added, "If I had daughters, I'd lock them up."

When we left, Sandy gave me a hug and there was my face, all up close and personal with her boobs. It felt like the perfect ending to a perfect day, even if she only laughed when I asked her for her phone number. Cosmo was in a great mood, too, because Amanda had accepted his offer of a lift home.

I got into the back of Cosmo's car, feeling like a million bucks.

I had no idea that just five minutes later, everything would come crashing down around me. And that this time the Higher Power was either helping someone else, or he'd gone to bed early.

Because this time, there would be no miracle.

This time, I was screwed.

24

E U B M R L

blur, bum, rum, rub, rube, lure, rule, mule, rue

R U M B L E

osmo pulled up outside our place just a few minutes later. Amanda got out of the passenger seat and yanked it forward, so I could climb out of the back. "Congrats again, kiddo," she said. "Your mom's going to be awfully proud of you."

Cosmo got out too and gave me a bear hug. "You rock, word nerd."

Amanda got back into the car. Cosmo was heading around to the driver's side when a voice came out of the darkness. "Cosmo."

Cosmo turned. Like some sort of ghoulish phantom, Silvio materialized from behind a tree. And he wasn't alone. Two other tough-looking guys flanked him, one on either side. They looked like the Three Stooges – only older, bigger, uglier, and way, way scarier.

"Silvio," said Cosmo calmly. "This isn't a good time."

"That's the problem, my friend. There never seems to be a good time."

"I've been busy –"

"I want my money."

"And you'll get it. I've already given you three hundred bucks."

"That's not even paying off the interest."

"C'mon Sil. I just got full-time work –"

"What's going on?" Amanda had gotten out of the car and was walking toward us.

"Amanda, wait in the car," said Cosmo.

"Who are these people?"

"Just a little misunderstanding."

Silvio sneered. "This your lady friend?" He turned to Amanda. "What's a sweet thing like you see in a scumbag like him?" He reached out to touch her arm and Cosmo whacked his hand away.

"Don't touch her."

Silvio's eyes flashed with anger. "She know about your previous occupation?"

"Yes, I do," Amanda said, trying to sound calm, but I could hear the quaver in her voice.

"And still she stays with you. Contrary to what some of your ex-girlfriends told me, you must be great in the sack." His buddies laughed.

"Shut up," I said. Actually I only meant to think it, but it popped out of my mouth.

Silvio and his goons turned and looked at me.

"What's with your midget friend, Cosmo? You develop a taste for boys when you were in prison?"

Cosmo took a step toward Silvio with his fists raised, but Goon Number One quickly moved in and held him back.

"You're high," said Cosmo, looking into Silvio's eyes.

"F— you," said Silvio.

"I'm gonna call the cops," I blurted, which, in retrospect, was not the best thing to say because Goon Number Two grabbed my arms and pinned them behind my back. I couldn't move and it hurt.

"Let him go," Cosmo said. "Let him and Amanda leave. They won't call anyone."

Silvio laughed. "I've tried to be generous to you, Cosmo. I've given you other options."

"And I've told you. I'm through with that life."

"Then I have no other choice but to show you how

serious I am about wanting my money," Silvio said, as he took a step closer to Cosmo.

Suddenly Amanda stepped right in between them, which I thought was really brave. "What does he owe you?"

"Two thousand bucks. With interest, it's more like twenty-five hundred."

"I can get you that money first thing tomorrow morning," said Amanda. "As soon as the banks open."

"Forget it, Amanda. I'm not taking your money," Cosmo said.

"You can pay me back," Amanda said. "Without interest."

"I have about a hundred and fifty bucks in quarters saved up," I piped in, thinking about my quarter jar. "It was supposed to go into my education fund, but you can have that, too."

"No. No one's bailing me out."

Suddenly, and without warning, Silvio punched Cosmo hard in the gut. Cosmo doubled over in pain. When he straightened up, Goon Number One punched him in the face. Cosmo tried to defend himself, but it was two against one. When Silvio punched him in the stomach again, Cosmo fell to the pavement.

Amanda screamed. I screamed. Goon Number Two, the guy who was holding me, put a big hairy hand over my mouth. I bit down hard and he let go, and I managed to squirm free. Then I leaped onto Silvio's back because he was raining down blows on Cosmo, who was still lying on the ground.

"Stop it, stop it!" I screamed, and I hit his head repeatedly with my MOST PROMISING NEWCOMER trophy. Finally he stood up and twisted his body back and forth, trying to get me off his back. As I hung on for dear life, I could see Goon Number One kicking Cosmo as he lay on the ground, and Amanda whacking the goon with her purse. Then Goon Number Two grabbed me from behind and pulled me off Silvio's back. I landed hard on the ground and my trophy flew out of my hand and hit the driveway.

Looking up, I saw the hose coiled up at the side of the house and I had an idea. I crawled over to it, grabbed the nozzle, and turned on the water full blast. I started spraying them all, trying to avoid Amanda and Cosmo, but that was easier said than done. And, if I'm totally honest, even though I was terrified, I felt more alive than I ever had in my whole life.

Suddenly sirens filled the night air. Next thing I knew, two cop cars pulled up out front. Silvio and his goons actually tried to make a run for it, but who were they kidding? The cops told all of us to get down on our knees and put our hands behind our heads, just like in the movies. Aside from me and the cops, everyone was drenched. Cosmo was really bashed up. A bunch of neighbors had gathered on the sidewalk to watch.

And that's pretty much what things looked like when, seconds later, my mom came home.

25

N M T Y O I E S T

toniest, noise, noisy, stony, moist, toes, totem, mittens

T E S T I M O N Y

Ambrose! Oh my God, what's going on, what happened?" My mom was almost screaming as she leapt out of the car. She wrapped her arms around me and held me tight.

"What the hell happened here?" she shouted at one of the cops. "Who are these men?" I don't think she recognized Cosmo, with his bruised and bloodied face.

"Ma'am, you're going to have to calm down," said a police officer.

"Calm down? *Calm down?*" she shrieked.

While Mom shouted at one cop, the other officers handcuffed Cosmo, Silvio, and the goons and put them in the backseats of the two cruisers. I guess they decided that Amanda and I weren't flight risks or hardened criminals because once my mom had calmed down a little, they told her (and Mr. Acheson, who'd dropped her off and who now stood on the sidewalk, looking very uncomfortable) that we could drive ourselves down to the station to give our statements.

Amanda couldn't drive Cosmo's car because it wasn't an automatic, so Mr. Acheson had to take us. Amanda and I got into the backseat of his brand-new Prius, a hybrid that ran on a combination of gas and electricity. I would have liked to ask him questions about this, but under the circumstances I decided against it.

As we drove, following the police cruisers at a respectable distance, Amanda, who was shaken, started talking to my mom.

"Ms. Bukowski, I don't even know where to begin. This is a terrible way to finally meet you."

"And you are?" my mom asked. Her voice was ice cold.

"Amanda. Amanda Svecova," she said. "Director of the West Side Scrabble Club."

My mom nodded in the front seat. "Huh. Interesting. The club I very clearly told my son he was not allowed to join."

"But – you signed the consent form," Amanda started, then she stopped. She looked at me, hard. I just turned away and stared out the window.

"I did no such thing. What kind of organization do you run, anyway?" my mom continued. "He's a minor. Did it even cross your mind to check with me?"

"No," Amanda said firmly, "it didn't. I took your son's word that he was telling me the truth." I could still feel her eyes boring into me like a drill. "I believed I could trust him. Clearly I was mistaken."

"Well, I can't imagine that the game of Scrabble had anything to do with what I witnessed tonight. I have no idea what you were doing anywhere near our thug of a neighbor –"

"Surely you're not referring to Cosmo," said Amanda, but my mom just cut her off.

"I'm not talking to you. I'm talking to my son."

"Mom, Cosmo didn't do anything wrong. . . ."

She laughed, but there was nothing *ha-ha* about it.

"Your son's telling the truth," said Amanda, and I could hear the edge in her voice. "Cosmo's been nothing but a friend to Ambrose. A father figure . . ."

Oh, man.

"Don't you ever call that . . . that convict creep a father figure."

A cold silence fell.

Finally Amanda said, her voice tight with anger, "Alright, I'll make a deal with you. I won't call Cosmo a father figure if you won't call him a creep. He's working really hard to put his life back on track."

"Is he your boyfriend?" Mom asked. "If so, I pity your taste in men."

I hazarded a glance at Amanda. She looked like she wanted to reach forward and tear out my mom's hair.

"How dare you say such a thing!"

"I'm just calling it as I see it."

"Now, Irene, easy does it," Bob said, the first words I'd heard him say all evening.

"You stay out of this," Mom snapped.

I felt kind of sorry for Bob, all of a sudden.

We arrived at the police station. It was a huge building, housing the main division for the whole city of Vancouver. Bob found a parking spot on the street and we all got out of the car. Amanda was so angry, she was vibrating.

"I'm beginning to see why your son has such difficulty telling you the truth, Ms. Bukowski. Because it wouldn't make any difference to you, would it? You'd still believe exactly what you want to believe." Then she looked at me and said, "Good luck, Ambrose. I can see you're going to need it." She strode off alone toward the cop shop.

I'd never been inside a police station before. All I knew about cop shops I'd learned from watching reruns of "Barney Miller," when we lived in Regina.

The reality was quite different. This one was much busier than the world of "Barney Miller," but big and clean and somehow efficient and businesslike all at once.

We sat in a large waiting room, with bucket seats and fluorescent lighting and lousy magazines. It was full of people from all walks of life. I think I saw a lady who was really a man, but I don't know for sure.

A nice uniformed policeman, whose name tag read SERGEANT JAMES, came and got me. My mom insisted on coming, too. He took us back to a little glassed-in office that overlooked the bustle of the station. Mr. Acheson stayed in the waiting area. I got the feeling he wished he could just go home.

"You say you'd been out with one of the gentlemen involved in the altercation – is that right?" Sergeant James began. He was taking my statement, and I have to admit, it felt kind of cool.

"Yes. Cosmo Economopoulos. I was with him all day."

My mom sucked in her breath. "Jesus Christ."

"Where had you been?"

"An all-day Scrabble tournament. I won six of my eight games."

"Congratulations," said Sergeant James, while Mom just stared daggers at him.

"Then we had dinner at Milestone's on West 4th. Which was delicious, by the way. I would highly recommend the fettuccine Alfredo, if you ever go there. It's peanut-free." I added that last part for my mom's benefit.

"Thanks for the tip. When you came home, what happened?"

"This friend of Cosmo's, well ex-friend, Silvio, was waiting for Cosmo with two big guys."

"Had you seen this fellow Silvio before?"

I nodded. "A couple of times."

"What?" That was my mom.

"Ms. Bukowski, please," said Sergeant James. "Can you tell me about these other times?"

"Well, once I overheard him asking Cosmo for some money he owed him. And another time I didn't see him, but there was a brick through Cosmo's front window and we were pretty sure we knew who did it. He was sending a message."

My mom sucked in her breath again. "You told me that was some neighborhood kids."

"We didn't want you or the Economopouloses to worry."

"We?"

I knew the heaping piles of you-know-what that I would be in later, but here's the thing: It was kind of a good feeling to be asked all these questions. To be the center of attention. It was like I was a guest on a talk show, and someone was really interested in what I had to say. Also, he was a police officer and I felt obligated to tell the truth. And even though my mom was sitting right beside me, it was easier to look a policeman in the eye and tell him all this stuff than it ever would have been to look her in the eye and tell her.

"What about the second time?"

I hesitated. "He came knocking on our door one night, when Mom was at work."

"Oh my God. Oh my God, oh my God," Mom started chanting, as she rocked back and forth in her seat.

"Did he threaten you?"

"Sort of. He'd figured out I wasn't Cosmo's nephew."

"Cosmo was pretending you were his nephew?" Mom was practically shrieking.

"No, no, that was just a little something I made up so Silvio would leave the first time I saw him and so Cosmo would drive me to the Scrabble Club. You see,"

I said to Sergeant James, "he didn't want to take me, even though he liked playing Scrabble himself. It involved some convincing. But then he met Amanda, who's giving a statement to your colleague, I believe, and he was totally googly-eyed about her, so getting a drive was not a problem after that."

"How many times have you been in his car?" my mom asked.

I shrugged. "Ten? Twenty?"

She kind of moaned and sank in her seat.

"So this Silvio threatened you," said Sergeant James, trying to bring us back on topic.

"Sort of," I said. "I mean, it wasn't anything he said; it was the way he said it. He said to tell Cosmo to pay him what he owes him, or else."

"So Cosmo owed Silvio money," said Sergeant James.

"Yeah. See, Silvio and Cosmo used to work together when Cosmo was a druggie and a thief. They were friends back then. And Silvio loaned Cosmo some money – two thousand dollars – and before Cosmo could pay him back, he was arrested after he tripped on a Labradoodle, but when he got out of jail, Silvio still wanted his money, even though Cosmo took the fall for him in a way because Silvio was also supposed to be in on the Labradoodle job. But Cosmo didn't have the money because, well, he'd been in jail, and then at first when he got out, he was just lazy. But then he did get a job, but they didn't give him a lot of shifts at first so he didn't earn a lot of money, and he was trying to pay Silvio back a little bit at a time, but Silvio didn't think it was fast enough."

Mom buried her head in her hands.

"But Cosmo could have got the money if he wanted to, I'm sure of it. He could have borrowed it from his parents, or from Amanda. She offered to give them the money tonight, in fact, and I offered to give him my quarter collection, which was supposed to go into my education fund."

"You didn't," my mom said, her head still in her hands.

"No, I didn't, because Cosmo wouldn't let me. And he wouldn't let Amanda, either. That's the thing. He's a very honorable guy. . . ."

Now Mom snorted. "Honorable? What kind of 'honorable' person would start up a friendship with a twelve-year-old boy?"

"Mom, he's not a pervert."

She turned to Sergeant James. "I want you to arrest this man for . . . for kidnapping a minor . . . for whatever it is he had in his sick head –"

"Mom!"

She turned to me. "Did he touch you? Did he say things to you? Did he take pictures of you?"

"Mom, stop! He's a good guy. He's my best friend."

She looked at Sergeant James again. "Help me out here, I'm begging you."

Sergeant James shrugged. "Nothing the kid says leads me to believe . . ." She gave him the biggest stink-eye I'd ever seen. "But if you want, I can ask him a few routine questions."

"You can't do that!" I said, my voice rising. "That's just insulting. Why can't you take my word for it, Mom? Why can't you believe a word I say?"

She turned her stink-eye on me. "You're asking me why I can't believe a word you say? You have the gall to ask me that, after everything you've just said in here?"

She did have a point.

"I think that's everything for now," said Sergeant James. He stood up, signaling that the interview was over. "I may need to ask you more questions at another time, Ambrose, but for now you're free to go."

"What about Cosmo?"

"He'll be spending the night in lockup."

"But it wasn't his fault –"

"It's just routine."

"Will they let him see a doctor? Those guys really hurt him."

"Don't worry. He'll be looked after."

"Let's go, Ambrose," Mom said.

"Please don't charge him with anything. All he's trying to do is lead a regular life."

"Now," my mom said firmly. She grabbed my arm and marched me toward Bob, who was wedged in between two women who looked a lot like prostitutes, if you ask me. Amanda was nowhere to be seen.

I thought I saw the sarge give me a sympathetic wave as we left.

Bob dropped us off and drove away pretty fast. Mom hadn't been very nice to him on the drive home, saying things like "Don't stick your nose where it doesn't belong." Once she actually said, "Shut up, Bob," even though saying "shut up" in our household was a big no-no.

The Economopouloses' Escort was parked out front. As we walked up the driveway, Mr. and Mrs. E hurried out of their house, still dressed up from their evening out.

"We just got a call from Cosmo. He's at the police station."

"I know, we were just there too. I saw the whole thing," I said.

Mrs. E's eyes widened. "Are you alright?"

"No, he's not alright," my mom said coldly.

"I'm fine," I said.

"Your son has been a terrible influence," said my mom.

"He has not," I protested.

"Ambrose, get in the house. Now." Mom grabbed my arm and started to pull me away.

"We go to see Cosmo now," Mr. E said.

"My baby," Mrs. E added, and she dabbed her eyes with a handkerchief.

"Baby, my ass," muttered Mom, which, even under the circumstances, was unnecessarily rude.

"None of it was Cosmo's fault," I shouted, as the Economopouloses got into their car and backed it out of the driveway.

And that's when I saw it.

My MOST PROMISING NEWCOMER trophy, lying right where the front left tire of the Escort had been. The little silver cup was crushed into a gazillion pieces.

"What's that?" my mom asked.

"It's nothing," I said.

I picked up the pieces and tossed them into the bushes.

— 26 —

E N R L I B O L E

brine, brillo, loner, bile, lore, robe, rob, bone, lion

R E B E L L I O N

When we got inside, Mom asked me to tell her everything. Having told the worst of it at the police station, I figured I might as well come one hundred percent clean. So I did tell her everything, from start to finish. On the one hand, it felt good to get it all off my chest because I wasn't used to keeping so many secrets from her. On the other hand, I wasn't so dumb as to think that my belated honesty would suddenly make everything A-OK.

When I was finished, she was quiet for a long time.

"I can't believe that you lied to me like that. Over and over again."

I didn't know what to say. "Sorry" seemed pretty lame.

"You never used to lie. We used to tell each other everything. Then we moved to Vancouver and, for some reason, that all changed."

It was like she was talking to herself more than to me. I couldn't hold back a huge yawn; it was one o'clock in the morning and it had been a long day.

"You're exhausted. We'll pick this up in the morning." She stood and held out her hand to help me off the couch.

I went to bed and lay under my Buzz Lightyear sheets, staring up at the glow-in-the-dark stars on my ceiling.

Then I turned to the photo of my dad. "I'm sorry if I've disappointed you," I whispered.

I knew I wouldn't sleep a wink.

Next thing I remembered, sunlight was streaming in through my basement window and my clock read 11:00 A.M. I'd slept like a log for ten hours straight.

When I wandered into our living room, Mom wasn't there. I looked in her room, but she wasn't there either. I felt a sudden rush of panic and I yelled out "Mommy?"

like a five-year-old. I kind of looked like a five-year-old too, standing there in my rocket-ship pajamas, which were way too small for me now and even had a new hole right by my you-know-what.

But then there she was, walking through the front door. I was flooded with relief, but only for a moment because I saw how grim she looked.

"You're up," she said.

"Were you out shopping?"

She shook her head. "I was upstairs, talking to the Economopouloses."

"About what? Is Cosmo okay? Is he home?"

She started tidying up things that didn't need tidying, like moving a cushion an inch or two, and lifting up a plant, then putting it right back down in the same spot. "I don't know, nor do I care, about where Cosmo is or how he is. I was giving our notice."

My heart sank. I knew what "giving notice" meant because we'd done it over and over again – in Calgary, in Edmonton, in Regina, and in Kelowna. It meant that we were leaving.

"Where are we going?"

"I've been making some calls," she said. "Apparently they need sessionals in English lit at the University of Manitoba, in Winnipeg."

"Winnipeg?"

"Who knows, maybe this time I'll get lucky and be offered a full-time position." She looked almost hopeful.

"But why?"

"I'm surprised that you even need to ask me that."

"What about Bob? I thought you liked him."

She shrugged. "Your well-being is far more important to me than any man."

"Mom, please. My well-being is weller than it's ever been. And I'm sorry I lied, unbelievably, enormously sorry, but I don't want to move again –"

"What you want is irrelevant, Ambrose. You clearly can't be trusted to make reasonable decisions on your own behalf, so I have to make them for both of us."

"But I have friends here. Real friends. Not just Cosmo and Amanda, but all the Scrabble Club people."

"Ambrose, those people aren't your friends. I saw a documentary once about people who join Scrabble Clubs. More often than not, they're a bunch of misfits."

"You haven't even met them! And has it ever crossed your mind that I'm a misfit?"

"Don't say that about yourself."

"And that every time we go somewhere else and I have to try to start over, I fit in even less? And this time, finally, I've met some people who accept me for me, and I don't care if they're older or whatever."

"Well, I care. . . ."

"You know what I think?" I shouted. "I think you like it when I don't have friends because then all I have is you, and it's just you and me against the world. And maybe that's why you want us to leave again because I'm finally happy, Mom, I'm happy! But maybe you'd rather I be miserable, like you. So instead, we're going to keep moving and twenty years from now, I'll be a total loser who still lives at home with you, but maybe that's what you want. Because it's the only way you'll have a piece of Dad with you forever."

By now tears were rolling down my face, and I must've looked totally pathetic in my rocket-ship pajamas with one testicle peeping through, but I was beyond caring. Then I saw that my mom was crying too.

"That is a terrible thing to say."

Maybe it was, but I couldn't help it. The words just came flooding out, words that had been there, hiding, for a long, long time. "I think you've gotten so used to being miserable, it's just easier to stay that way. It's just easier not to trust anyone, to just keep to yourself and drink too much wine all the time. And I feel sorry for Dad because it must make him so sad to see what a bitter bitch you've become."

She slapped me hard across the face.

I was going to make a run for the door, but even though I was more emotional than I'd ever been in my whole life, I still had enough sense to remember that

a) I was in my pajamas and b) that you could see one of my nuts. So instead I ran into my bedroom, which was anticlimactic since I didn't have a door and beads don't slam.

I waited for my mom to come in and apologize for the slap because she had never, ever hit me before. But instead, I heard our front door open and close.

After a few minutes, I got up and went into the living room. She'd left me a note that read, "Gone out to clear my head. Back in an hour." She'd written an *XO* at the bottom of the note because we'd made a vow to each other years ago to never leave mad.

I gazed at the note. Then I walked back into my room and got changed into my purple cords and a T-shirt. I rummaged around for the backpack I'd used for school and filled it with two pairs of underwear, one pair of socks, one T-shirt, a rain jacket, and my library book. I tried to stuff my dad's sweater in too, but it wouldn't fit, so I tied it around my waist.

Then I went into the kitchen and used up almost a whole loaf of spelt bread, making cheese sandwiches. I filled a big water bottle and placed it in its own pouch at the side of the pack. My EpiPen went into the outer pouch. I found an old sleeping bag in the closet. It wouldn't fit into the backpack either, so I grabbed a canvas shopping bag and put it into that instead.

I was just about to leave when I thought of three more things.

I took our Scrabble board from the shelf and stuck it into the canvas shopping bag next to the sleeping bag. Then I went back into my bedroom and got my quarter collection out from under the bed. I poured as much of it as I could carry into my backpack's hidden inner pouch. Last but not least, I grabbed the photo of my dad from my bedside table and wedged it gently between the sleeping bag and the Scrabble game.

Then I tied up my Ikes and walked out, locking the door behind me.

I dropped my backpack behind the same tree Silvio had hidden behind only last night, then I knocked on the Economopouloses' door. Mrs. E answered. She'd been crying. I kind of threw myself at her and we hugged each other for a long time. "Oh, Ambrose," she said, "I'm going to miss you so much."

"Me, too."

I cried a little as she squeezed me tight, then I asked her if Cosmo was back.

"Not yet," she said. "He seemed okay, but I'm worried for him."

"It'll be alright," I said. "He didn't do anything wrong."

She nodded and blew her nose into her handkerchief. "But, sometimes, when somebody's done something wrong before . . . they think he'll do it again."

"Yeah, but there were witnesses. Me and Amanda."

She sniffed again. "She called me this morning. Such a nice girl. And you, you're such a nice boy."

I told her I'd see her later, then I grabbed my backpack from its hiding spot. I walked down to the bus stop at Bayswater and West 4th Avenue and, a few minutes later, I boarded the number four.

I didn't know where I was going. I didn't know what I was doing. I only knew that I wasn't moving again. If mom really wanted to leave, she'd have to leave without me.

27

W N Y R A U A

ray, way, ran, wary, raw, war, warn, yawn, run, away

R U N A W A Y

iguring out where to go wasn't easy. It wasn't like I had an army of friends to choose from. Cosmo was still in jail. Amanda might still be mad at me, and even if she wasn't, she'd probably feel obligated to call my mom. I didn't know where Mohammed or Joan lived, and besides, I couldn't really ask them to harbor a fugitive.

I had to face it. If I was doing this, I was doing it alone.

I knew I didn't want to wind up downtown with the other homeless kids on Granville Street because I'd seen them when I'd been down there with my mom. They were tough and they hung out in packs and a lot of them had dogs and body piercings and tattoos, while I had Spiderman underwear and a Scrabble board. I just couldn't see it being a good fit.

I could catch a Greyhound bus to another town in BC, or to Calgary to see Nana Ruth, but that would defeat the purpose, since the whole point was that I wanted to stay in Vancouver.

Then I had an idea, and a pretty good one at that. I jumped off the bus after only about six stops.

I would go to live on an island.

Granville Island.

A fifteen-minute bus ride from my home.

28

N T O I U S L O

slit, lost, not, soot, suit, lotion, sun, nut, loot, loon, lust

S O L U T I O N

ince it was only one o'clock in the afternoon when I arrived on Granville Island, walking from the bus stop and along the road that traveled under the Granville Street Bridge, I had a lot of time to kill. Lucky for me, it was a beautiful day, so I spent a couple of hours on a bench by the water, eating two of my cheese sandwiches and reading *Inkspell* and dozing in the sunshine. Then I took out a bunch of my quarters and paid to go into the Miniature Train Museum. I'd been there only once before, but it was a great place, especially the working model train set with its own separate room. The man who ran it didn't seem to mind that I stayed for a long time, and he told me all about the different model ships and planes that he also had on display.

I spent the rest of my afternoon and evening watching the buskers perform for money, including a sword swallower and an excellent magician who used me as an assistant for one of his tricks. It felt nice being among the throngs of locals and tourists enjoying their Sunday, although, to be honest, all my gear was getting a little heavy to lug around, especially my quarters.

Since it was mid-May, it didn't get really dark until close to ten o'clock. But when it did get dark, the feeling on the island changed. It didn't feel super dangerous or anything, just . . . lonely, even though there were still quite a few people around, enjoying the restaurants and theaters.

But by midnight most people had cleared out, and I had that overwhelming feeling again that I was a mere speck in the universe. It wasn't a terrible sensation, or even a depressing one, just, I don't know, sort of profound and true, and it made me kind of melancholy. I sat down by the water's edge and looked at all the lights shining brightly in the buildings downtown. I thought about all the people going about their lives in those buildings, and I thought about my mom, who, by now, was probably worried sick. I got up and found a pay phone by the visitor's center and used one of my quarters to call home.

She picked up halfway through the first ring. "Ambrose?" I could hear the fear in her voice.

"Hi, Mom."

"Oh, thank God, Ambrose, where are you?"

"I can't tell you."

"Is someone telling you to say that? Just answer yes or no."

"I'm alone, Mom."

"Then let me come get you. We can talk —"

I hung up then because I'd seen enough movies to know that the police could trace my call if I stayed on too long. Then I wandered over to the water park, which hadn't opened for the summer season yet. I thought about pulling out my sleeping bag and camping out under some bushes for the night, but then I saw a bunch of homeless guys. They were setting up camp with their shopping carts near some other bushes nearby and even though they were probably harmless, like Preacher Paul, I didn't really want to stick around to find out.

So I walked to the far end of the island, past the Emily Carr School of Art to the Granville Island Hotel. It was a low-rise building, and if I was ever lucky enough to be able to stay in a hotel in my own city, I would choose this one because it looked so friendly and so quiet and so off the beaten path. The doorman was busy helping some people to their car, so I scooted inside. There were washrooms down a side corridor, and I slipped into the men's with my stuff.

It was warm in there, if a little smelly – a mix of disinfectant and pee. I locked myself into a stall and put the seat down on the toilet and did my best to get comfortable, unzipping my sleeping bag and wrapping it around me like a blanket. Then I took out the picture of my dad laughing and propped it up on the toilet tank.

"I wish Mom could remember the joke she told you to make you laugh so hard," I said to him, looking at his smiling face.

Then I closed my eyes and tried not to feel too scared as I settled in for the night.

It's not something I'd recommend to anyone, sleeping on a toilet. All night I drifted in and out of sleep, mostly out, and my body was sore and achy all over. About six o'clock, the washroom door banged open. I could see a cleaning lady's cart and a cleaning lady's feet. She was singing tunelessly to herself. I peered under the stall. She was a big cheerful-looking woman, and she was wearing an iPod. She didn't seem to notice that the last stall was occupied. When she entered the first stall to scrub the toilet, I jumped up and ran out, clutching my backpack and my shopping bag and the photo of my dad, my sleeping bag flapping around my shoulders like I was a superhero. I ran right out of the hotel and I was pretty sure that no one saw me leave.

So far so good, in my new life as a fugitive.

I ate two more cheese sandwiches and refilled my water bottle at the water park fountain, then at 6:50, I found the same pay phone I'd used to call my mom. Only this time I called the Economopouloses.

"Ambrose? Your mama, she's sick with worry," said Mrs. E, when she picked up the phone.

"Is Cosmo back?"

Suddenly he was on the line. "Ambrose, you idiot, where the hell are you?"

"Did they charge you?"

"No. They let me go with a warning."

"What about Silvio?"

"He had some outstanding warrants for his arrest. They're keeping him in till they set a trial date."

"Good."

"Now tell me where you are."

"I can't."

"Your mom's going crazy."

"I don't want to move."

"I know you don't."

"I have to hang up now, in case you're having my call traced."

"Ambrose, you watch too much TV. . . ."

I hung up.

I wandered over to the market, which was already showing signs of life, even though it was only seven o'clock. The shop owners were laying out their produce and trucks were making deliveries of fish and I could smell bread and cookies baking. It made me ravenous all over again and I sat down by the water's edge and ate my second-to-last cheese sandwich.

When the market officially opened at eight, I ducked into one of the public washrooms and carefully counted out five dollars in quarters and put them into my pocket. Then I went to a bakery and, after making the shopkeeper swear that there were no peanuts in anything, I bought an enormous blueberry muffin and an equally enormous chocolate chip cookie, since my mom wasn't around to tell me not to. I pocketed my change and took my treats outside.

While I ate them, I considered my options. I only had about fifty dollars in quarters left, and I knew they wouldn't last me very long, even if I only had to use them for food. I thought about stealing, but stealing just wasn't my style, and besides, it could get me arrested. I thought about garbage-picking or dumpster-diving, but that was simply too gross, and with my peanut allergy, it could also be deadly.

If I couldn't steal or pick garbage, I concluded that there was only one option left. I had to earn some money, which meant I had to get a job.

I went back inside the market and asked a few of the shopkeepers if they needed any help, but they either laughed at me or ignored me. One guy looked at me and my backpack and my canvas shopping bag suspiciously and said, "Where are your parents?"

"Shopping," I lied. "There they are now." I pointed to a couple strolling nearby and pretended to join them, before heading back outside.

I was stumped. *If I couldn't get a job, how could I make money?*

Then I glanced down and my eyes just happened to land on my Scrabble board, sticking out of the top of the canvas bag.

And that's when the lightbulb went on in my head. I had – if I do say so myself – a totally brilliant idea.

29

U E T D S B

debuts, bused, debts, tube, bed, dubs, best, duets, stub

BUSTED

By eleven o'clock the Granville Market was bustling, even though it was a Monday. Out back, facing the water, a magician had set up near one set of doors and a violin player near another. Crowds gathered around to watch them perform.

I picked an empty bench, right in between the magician and the violin player, and set up my Scrabble board. Then I pulled out a sign I'd made on a piece of cardboard from a recycling bin. SCRABBLE GAMES, FIVE

DOLLARS, it read. BEAT ME AND I WILL GIVE YOU YOUR FIVE DOLLARS BACK!

I had nothing to hang the sign on, so I simply held it up over my head. A lot of people wandered past and laughed at my sign, but not in a mean way. After about half an hour, when my arms were starting to ache, an older guy, probably in his fifties, stopped. He was with a young girl and he wore a sailor's cap.

"So you think you could beat an old pro like me at Scrabble?" he asked.

"Yes," I said.

"Well, we'll see about that, won't we, Ashley?" he said to the girl, and he handed her a five-dollar bill. "Why don't you hang on to the money, in case the Lilliputian here tries to scam us."

We played a game. People stopped to watch, especially when it became obvious that I was crushing the guy. He had this vein in his forehead that I swear I could see pulsing as I bingoed twice, blocked good spots for him to place words, and built multiple words on one turn.

I won, 320 to 252. "Beginner's luck," he said grudgingly. He stood up and started to walk away.

"Your daughter needs to give me my five dollars," I said.

I thought the vein in his forehead was going to pop. "She's not my daughter," he sputtered. "She's my girlfriend."

Ashley handed me my five dollars and he grabbed her arm and they hurried away. A few of the onlookers laughed, and a couple of them shoved loonies into my hand.

Then someone said, "Hey, I recognize you, Most Promising Newcomer." It was Sandy, my waitress from Milestone's, and she was with some friends. Maybe because she wasn't at work and therefore not looking for tips, she wore a baggy shirt that hid her beautiful boobs. But it was nice to see her anyway, and she gave me five dollars without even playing a game. More important, she didn't ask questions about who I was with, or why I had so much stuff with me.

Business wasn't exactly booming, but by three o'clock that afternoon, I'd played three games and had easily won them all. I was up over twenty bucks (including Sandy's five) and I was counting out my five-dollar bills plus the few extra loonies I'd been given. Just when I was thinking it wouldn't be so difficult to finance my new homeless existence, a policeman approached.

"Quite the operation you've got going here, son."

"Thank you," I said.

"Do you have a license?"

"For what?"

"To run your little business here."

"This isn't a business. It's a board game."

"All the buskers down here – that magician over there, that violin player – they all have to apply for a license from the city to perform in a public place."

"I'm not performing."

"No . . . but performing without a license is a lesser offense than gambling, which is technically what you're doing."

"It's just a game."

"But you're playing for money."

I quickly shoved my earnings into my pocket.

"Look, I don't want to give you a hard time, but I am going to have to ask you to pack it up."

I realized there was no point arguing with him. "Okay."

"Do your parents know what you're doing?"

"Yes."

"Well, they have an enterprising young son," he said, then he laughed.

I packed up my Scrabble board and shook the policeman's hand.

Then I walked to the other side of the market, to a square outside a building called the Loft, and set up my game and my sign on another bench.

The same policeman found me there less than half

an hour later. I was partway through a game with a big burly guy, who looked like he could be a pro-wrestler. This time the cop wasn't so friendly.

"Okay, kid. You're coming with me."

So I packed up again. And even though it was obvious I was going to beat him, the pro-wrestler guy didn't give me my five bucks.

The policeman marched me over to a little office near the information center. I made up my mind that he could use all sorts of interrogation techniques and I would not crack: He could bully me, threaten me, use sleep deprivation or Chinese water torture, but it would be like drawing blood from a stone.

My resolve lasted about five seconds. "What's your parents' phone number?" he said, and I told him.

Well, I sort of told him. He called the number I gave him, and when someone picked up at the other end, he said, "Cosmo Economopoulos? I have your son here with me. Ambrose."

A minute later he hung up. "Okay, kid. Your dad's on his way."

Thirty minutes later, Cosmo showed up. His face looked worse than it had the last time I'd seen him, because the bruises were in full bloom now. He sported a swollen lip and a black eye.

"Ambrose," he said, and he pulled me into a tight hug. "We were worried sick." Then, when he saw the cop staring at his bruised face, he said, "Fishing accident. The fish won."

The cop let us leave after he told me never to set up my Scrabble board on Granville Island again. We started walking to Cosmo's car.

"Fishing accident?" I said.

"It was the first thing that popped into my head."

"Thanks for coming to get me."

"I'm not going to lie to you, Ambrose. Your mom's waiting in the car."

I stopped walking. "Why did you do that?"

"She was at our place when you called. She's beside herself."

"Then, thanks for nothing. I'll see you later." I started to walk in the opposite direction, but Cosmo grabbed my arm.

"Ambrose," he said.

My eyes filled with tears, even though I didn't want them to. "I don't want to move again."

"I know that. Your mom knows that. I think she might be willing to listen."

So I started walking with him again. When we approached Cosmo's car, Mom leaped out. She gave me a suffocating hug. Her eyes were puffy and red.

"Thank God you're alright." She peppered me with questions, like where had I slept, what had I eaten, had anyone tried to hurt me.

"Mom," I said.

She stopped talking.

"I'm only coming home on one condition."

"What's that?"

"That you agree to have supper with the Economopouloses tonight. And that you agree to actually listen to what we all have to say and try to keep an open mind."

Okay, so maybe that was three conditions.

My mom opened her mouth to argue when a funny thing happened. Cosmo laid a hand gently on her arm. She turned and looked at him. Then she turned back to me and said, "Okay. I'll agree to that. Now, please. Let's go home."

Which I found kind of ironic because that's all I'd ever wanted to begin with: to go back to a place I could truly call home.

30

E E C P A

pace, cepe, cape, cap, ace, ape, pea, pee, pa

P E A C E

he sky is different here. More blue and more vast. I gaze up at it as my mom and I drive down the highway in a rental car.

It's my thirteenth birthday, July 19th.

It was almost exactly two months ago that I ran away to Granville Island. We had our dinner at the Economopouloses' that night, and Mr. and Mrs. E and Cosmo and Amanda were all waiting for us. They each had a turn at crushing me with hugs. When they finally stopped, my body felt bruised and tired but also good.

The dinner was delicious. Mrs. E had gone all out, and I stuffed myself with lamb and tsatziki and dolmades and salad and roasted lemony potatoes and her famous peanut-free baklava.

The conversation wasn't too bad either. It had its ups and downs, but my mom actually listened to what I had to say. I told her again how happy I was in Vancouver and in this apartment. I told her how much I loved the Economopouloses and the Scrabble Club and especially Cosmo, who'd taught me things that, whether she liked it or not, I needed to know. "Like how to stand up for myself," I said. "Like how to have more self-confidence, even when I feel like a speck."

What I didn't admit was, thanks to Cosmo, I was even thinking of retiring my purple cords. But he didn't need to know that. It would just go to his head.

I won't lie and say it was perfect. I could tell my mom was still having trouble with a lot of it. Cosmo tried to reassure her. "Ambrose is a really special kid, Irene. He's taught me things, too. He saw the possibility in me, which I wasn't seeing in myself. I feel lucky to count him as my friend."

That made Mrs. E cry and she pulled out her hanky and blew her nose, making a sound like a Canada goose. Then I looked at my mom and I saw that she was crying too.

"His father was like that," she said. "Always seeing the good in others. Always seeing the possibility."

That brought tears to Amanda's eyes, and even Cosmo looked all choked up. Then I started thinking about my dad and how it really did suck that I never got a chance to know him, and pretty soon we were all crying. Mr. E had to leave the table and watch sports in the other room because he couldn't take it anymore.

After dinner, all the grown-ups got drunk on ouzo. At first they were laughing a lot, but then they all got maudlin and embarrassing. Mom and Amanda apologized to each other, which seemed kind of phony to me because I could tell they still didn't like each other very much. Finally, at one o'clock in the morning, I had to drag my mom back to our apartment. As she tried to get her shoes on, she kept saying, "I love you guys," and her words were all mushy and slurred. Eventually she picked up her shoes and walked back to our apartment barefoot.

The next morning she told me we weren't moving to Winnipeg, or to anywhere else for that matter. She also told me that if I ever pulled a stunt like running away again, or any other extreme tactic to get my own way, she would have me drawn and quartered.

I could safely say, this was an idle threat.

There are a lot of things that are still hard for my mom. Like thinking about me driving with Cosmo, whom she still doesn't totally trust. She's asked me to always sit in the backseat with my seat belt tightly fastened, and on the driver's side because, apparently, it's the passenger side that gets hit more often. I've promised, and so has Cosmo. I can't help but notice that every time she sees him, she always checks out his eyes to see if he's high. I'm pretty sure Cosmo's noticed it too, but he never says a word.

She's also made me promise not to go back to the climbing gym until she can afford to take me there and see it for herself. And every time we go into a restaurant, she still has to lecture the staff about my allergy, which I guess I'm kind of happy about because it saves me the trouble of doing it.

But she doesn't hold my hand when we cross Broadway anymore, and she's agreed that I can keep going to the Scrabble Club. She even came once, getting Jane to cover her summer-school classes so she could check it out. When she watched me play, I could tell she was really proud of me, especially when some of the other players told her how much they liked having me around.

Last night (the day before my birthday), I came home from picking up my first very own deodorant stick at the drugstore on Broadway because Mom and I had agreed that I kind of needed it. I walked into our apartment and almost had a heart attack when Mom, Cosmo, Amanda, and Mr. and Mrs. E all jumped up from behind the couch and yelled, "Surprise! Happy Birthday!" Mom had made a massive cake, and Mr. E grilled hot dogs and hamburgers on the barbecue in the yard. Mr. and Mrs. E gave me a check for fifty dollars, and Nana Ruth sent me another check for twenty, so altogether I had seventy bucks. Amanda and Cosmo gave me a Franklin, a sort of calculator for Scrabble players. You can punch in your letters and the Franklin will list all the words you can make. You can't use it during a game, but it's a great way to review your plays afterward.

"We have one more gift for you, too," Amanda said, as I was trying out the Franklin. She reached into her purse and pulled out a brand-new MOST PROMISING NEWCOMER trophy, identical to the first one. I gave it a place of honor beside the photo of my dad on my bedside table.

Just before we cut the cake, Bob showed up. He and my mom hadn't seen each other for a few weeks after the cooking class, but one night I heard Mom talking to him in a low voice on the phone and I'm pretty sure she was apologizing. Bob even brought me a gift. It was a book called *The Catcher in the Rye,* which sounds like a baseball book, but Bob tells me it isn't.

And Mom gave me this: a road trip to Calgary. We left early this morning. When we get there, we're going to stay with Nana Ruth. Then I'm going to play in the Calgary Scrabble Tournament. Mom, Cosmo, and Amanda entered me weeks ago, without telling me. We're going to spend some time camping in the Rockies too, after the tournament. My mom's even packed her camera, so she can take some nature photos. And for the first time ever, I'm going to see where my dad is buried, and while it may sound weird, that's the part I'm looking forward to most.

"The joke I was telling your father," she says to me now.

I look at her, confused.

"The photo you have in your bedroom. You've always wondered what joke I'd told him to make him laugh like that."

"Yeah."

"Knock, knock."

"Who's there?"

"Little old lady."

I groaned. "You've got to be kidding me."

"I'm telling you the joke; at least play along."

"Fine. Little old lady who?"

"I didn't know you could yodel."

"And Dad laughed at that?" But even as I said it, I realized I was laughing, too.

Mom smiled. "Dad and I laughed all the time. The quality of the joke was beside the point."

"Then have I got some knock-knock jokes for you. Knock, knock."

"Who's there?"

"Orange."

"Orange who?"

"Orange you glad you're my friend?"

When I'm through telling her my top ten lamest knock-knock jokes, I turn around in my seat and look out the rear window. Cosmo and Amanda are in his Camaro behind us. They're going to play in the tournament too, then head straight back to Vancouver because they both have to work.

I wave at Cosmo for the millionth time that day. And for the millionth time that day, he waves back.

E E H D N T

then, dent, hen, net, thee, teen, heed, ten

THE END

S O Y L S G A R

glossy, grassy, gross, royal, yoga, glassy, gory, gassy

G L O S S A R Y

(Not all of these words are found in traditional diction-
aries, but they are all found in the *Official Scrabble
Tournament and Club Word List.*)

Aa – rough, cindery lava

Anthem – song of praise

Culti – a cult

Exanthem – a skin eruption

Jive – type of jazz or swing music

Legume – a plant of the pea family

Mementos – things that serve as a reminder of
the past

Miaous – meows

Opossum – an arboreal mammal

Orach – a plant with edible spinach-like leaves

Pithy – concise

Potash – a potassium compound

Qi – "breath" in Chinese

Qwertys – a standard typewriter keyboard

Sh – used to urge silence

Taxon – a unit of scientific classification

Urethane – a crystalline compound

Whimsy – an impulsive or fanciful idea

Yegg – a burglar